YORK NOTES

General Editors: Professor A.N. Jeffares (*Universiy of Stirling*) & Professor Suheil Bushrui (*American University of Beirut*)

Brian Friel

TRANSLATIONS

Notes by Loreto Todd

MA (BELFAST) MA PH D (LEEDS)
Reader in International English, University of Leeds

LONGMAN
YORK PRESS

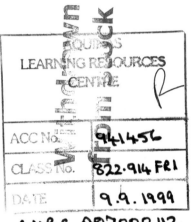
Excerpt from John Montague's poem "A Grafted Tongue' used by kind permission of the author and The Gallery Press. It is taken from his *Collected Poems* (1995).

YORK PRESS
Immeuble Esseily, Place Riad Solh, Beirut

PEARSON EDUCATION LIMITED
Edinburgh Gate, Harlow,
Essex CM20 2JE, United Kingdom
Associated companies, branches and representatives
throughout the world

First published 1996
Fourth impression 1999

ISBN 0–582–29348–0

Phototypeset by Gem Graphics, Trenance, Mawgan Porth, Cornwall
Printed in Singapore (PH)

Contents

Part 1: Introduction   *page* 5
   Brian Friel, the person   5
   Brian Friel, the writer   5
   Brian Friel's Irish heritage   7
   Brief historical background   7
   The linguistic history of Ireland   10
   Friel, Steiner and translation   14
   The title of the play   15
   The setting for *Translations*   17
   The problem of presenting two speech communities   17
   A note on the text   18

Part 2: Summaries   19
   General summary of *Translations*   19
   Detailed summaries   20

Part 3: Commentary   62
   Background   62
   Naming   62
   Naming characters   62
   Structure   65
   Characters   66
   Significance of the Famine   75
   Significance of the setting   75
   General comments   76

Part 4: Hints for study   77
   How to approach the play   77
   How to analyse plays   77
   How to write about *Translations*   78
   Answering questions on *Translations*   81
   Sample questions and suggested answers   81
   Revision questions   86
   Topics for classroom discussion   88

Part 5: Suggestions for further reading   91
The author of these notes   92

Part 1

Introduction

Brian Friel, the person

Brian Friel was born in Omagh, County Tyrone, Northern Ireland on 5 January 1929. His father, who was a teacher, was from Derry and his mother from an Irish-speaking area of Donegal. The family moved back to Derry City in 1939 when his father was appointed to a teaching job in Long Tower School. Friel first attended this school, before moving on to the local grammar school for boys, St Columb's College.

In 1945, Friel decided that he wanted to train for the Catholic priesthood and entered St Patrick's College, Maynooth, Co. Kildare, now a constituent College of the University of Ireland. At the time he was enrolled, the College was solely involved in training young men for the priesthood. After three years, it was clear that he would not be able to become a priest, so he left Maynooth and trained as a teacher at St Joseph's Teachers' Training College, Belfast. This institute was also single sex and Friel's segregated education may have had an effect on his knowledge of, and attitude towards, female characters.

In 1950, Friel became a school teacher in Derry, and for the next ten years he taught in primary and secondary schools and wrote in his spare time. He published a number of short stories in *The New Yorker*, wrote two radio plays which were broadcast by the BBC in 1958, and published a stage play, *A Doubtful Paradise*, in 1959. By 1960, he had sufficient confidence in his ability to give up teaching to work full time as a writer. He and his family moved to Donegal, where he still lives.

Brian Friel, the writer

Brian Friel has published prose fiction as well as drama. His best stories are collected in *The Saucer of Larks* (Victor Gollancz, London, 1962), *The Gold in the Sea* (Victor Gollancz, London, 1966), *Selected Stories* (The Gallery Press, Dublin, 1979) and *The Diviner: the Best Stories of Brian Friel* (The O'Brien Press, Dublin, 1983). His stories, like his plays, often deal with the inter-related themes of love, loyalty and family relationships, attitudes to home and exile, the bond between the individual and the community, language and identity, politics and power, poverty, oppression and violence. His stories have been well received but Friel's literary eminence relies mainly on his plays.

He has and had a very clear vision of the role of the dramatist in Ireland. Writing in the *Times Literary Supplement* (17 March 1972) he discussed Irish theatre audiences in the early part of the twentieth century and claimed:

> ... we recognised then that the theatre was an important social element that not only reflected but shaped the society it served; that the dramatists were revolutionary in the broadest sense of the word; and that subjective truth – the artist's truth – was dangerously independent of church and state.

Like many writers, he has realised that his audience could be both national and international:

> ... the world has become much smaller and we should now view ourselves not in an insular but in a world context ... The canvas can be as small as you wish, but the more accurately you write and the more truthful you are the more validity your play will have for the world.
> (Des Hickey and Gus Smith: *A Paler Shade of Green*
> (Leslie Frewin, London, 1972) p. 223)

Friel has been a relatively prolific dramatist, producing twenty plays over a thirty-year period. His plays are as follows:

The Enemy Within, first performed in Dublin, 1962
Philadelphia, Here I Come!, first performed in Dublin, 1964
The Loves of Cass McGuire, first performed in New York, 1966
Lovers, first performed in Dublin, 1967
Crystal and Fox, first performed in Dublin, 1968
The Mundy Scheme, first performed in Dublin, 1969
The Gentle Island, first performed in Dublin, 1971
The Freedom of the City, first performed in Dublin, 1973
Volunteers, first performed in Dublin, 1975
Living Quarters, first performed in Dublin, 1977
Aristocrats, first performed in Dublin, 1979
Faith Healer, first performed in New York, 1979
Translations, first performed in Derry, 1980
Three Sisters, first performed in Derry, 1981
The Communication Cord, first performed in Derry, 1982
Fathers and Sons, first performed in London, 1987
Making History first performed in Derry, 1988
Dancing at Lughnasa, first performed in Dublin, 1990
The London Vertigo, first performed in Dublin, 1992
Molly Sweeney, first performed in New York, 1996.

Translations, critically acclaimed throughout the English-speaking world, remains one of his most popular plays.

Brian Friel's Irish heritage

Friel was born into a Catholic community in Northern Ireland at a time when being a Catholic automatically meant being less privileged. He was, however, different from most of his Catholic contemporaries in two main ways: he was urban whereas most Catholics were rural and, because of his father's position, he was 'middle class' when most Catholics were manual workers. His life, however, spans many of the crucial events in the history of modern Ireland: he was born into a divided Ireland in a part of the country where many of his co-religionists found themselves more in sympathy with their Irish counterparts in the Irish Free State than with their British neighbours in Northern Ireland; he has lived through two major IRA campaigns (1950s and 1970s), aimed at forcing the British government to renegotiate the Treaty (of 1922) that had partitioned Ireland; he saw thousands of British troops stationed in Northern Ireland; and he lived through killings and bombings on a scale not seen in western Europe since the Second World War.

Friel's parents knew Irish Gaelic: his father had learnt it at school; his mother had grown up in an area of Donegal where it was still the main mother tongue; Friel himself learned it at school and, during his lifetime, he saw Irish Gaelic consistently lose ground to English. The loss of a language and the cultural deprivation that follows such a loss were to become thematic in his writings.

Brief historical background

To understand more fully the themes in Friel's plays and the underlying assumptions of his work, some historical background may be helpful. England's first serious attempt to conquer Ireland began in 1155 when the English Pope, Adrian IV (Nicholas Breakspeare), gave Henry II permission to take over Ireland in order to carry out religious reforms. The Anglo-Norman invasion that followed was thorough. It is estimated that by 1175 almost half of Ireland was subjugated, and an additional quarter had been added by 1250.

English authority was confined mainly to the urban centres in the east and south of Ireland and this authority declined during the fourteenth century. The decline was partly due to the difficulties of maintaining an effective military presence and partly to the fact that the early settlers gradually adopted the Irish language and Irish customs. By 1578, the Lord Chancellor Gerrarde complained: '. . . all English, and the most part with delight, even in Dublin, speak Irish, and greatly are spotted in manners, habit and conditions with Irish stains . . .'

The Tudor queens Mary and Elizabeth set in train a second conquest of Ireland and this, together with the Cromwellian routing of the Irish between 1649 and 1651, began the phase which resulted in the entire island coming under the jurisdiction of England. Donegal, where *Translations* is set, is one of the nine counties of Ulster and, since Ulster was seen as the greatest potential danger to English rule, it was singled out to be transformed into a stronghold of English law. The transformation was to be achieved by settling large numbers of Protestants, who were loyal to the throne, throughout the nine counties of Ulster.

It would be impossible to provide a detailed account of the relationship between England and Ireland over the last 400 years, but the following facts will provide the reader with some of the more significant dates and

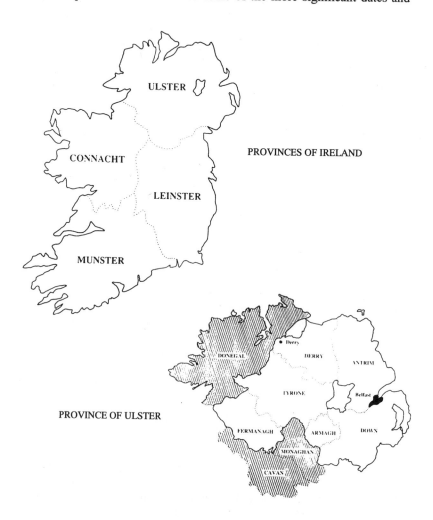

PROVINCES OF IRELAND

ULSTER

CONNACHT

LEINSTER

MUNSTER

PROVINCE OF ULSTER

DONEGAL

DERRY

ANTRIM

Derry

TYRONE

Belfast

FERMANAGH

ARMAGH

DOWN

MONAGHAN

CAVAN

events, relating to Northern Ireland in particular. It should be remembered that Friel's play was written at the height of the recent IRA campaign to reunite the six counties of Northern Ireland with the twenty-six counties of the Republic of Ireland.

1550	English settlements ('Plantations') in Ireland begin
1554	Mary Tudor, a Catholic, becomes Queen
1558	Elizabeth, a Protestant, succeeds Mary
1595	Hugh O'Neill, Earl of Tyrone, declares war on Elizabeth
1601	Hugh O'Neill defeated at Kinsale
1607	Flight of the Earls: Irish nobility find refuge in Europe
1608	Major Plantation of Ulster
1649–51	Cromwellian campaign results in massacre of Catholics
1689	Siege of Derry: Protestant defenders withstand James II's attack
1690	Battle of the Boyne: William of Orange defeats James II
1795	Penal Laws against Dissenters, i.e. against all who were not members of the established church
1798	'98 Rebellion: Presbyterians and Catholics united to fight the Penal Laws
1800	Act of Union: Ireland integrated into Britain
1829	Catholic Emancipation brought about largely through the efforts of Daniel O'Connell, 'the Liberator'
1831	Establishment of National Schools where English was to be the sole medium of education
1845–7	The Great Hunger: the potato famine kills about one third of the population and triggers mass emigration
1886	Gladstone's first Home Rule Bill: intends to establish a Parliament in Dublin; bill is defeated
1893	Gaelic League Movement: attempts to revive Irish Gaelic and to make Ireland independent
1905	Sinn Fein (= Ourselves Alone) Movement
1912	Home Rule Bill: Ulster Volunteer Force (UVF) founded by Edward Carson to keep Ulster British
1914	The First World War: Home Rule Bill suspended
1916	Easter Rising, an Irish insurrection against British rule: leaders executed
1918	All-Ireland Elections: clear mandate for independence
1919–21	War between England and Ireland
1921	'Anglo-Irish Treaty': Ireland to be subdivided, 26 counties to form 'Irish Free State', 6 northern counties to remain British
1922–3	Civil War in the Irish Free State as a result of the Treaty
1925	Partition of Ireland confirmed in Dublin and London
1948	Irish Free State declares itself a Republic
1956–62	Irish Republican Army (IRA) campaign in Northern Ireland

1968	Civil Rights Campaign launched in Northern Ireland addressing discrimination against Catholics in housing, employment and political rights
1969	Violence in Northern Ireland: British troops deployed
1971	Internment without trial: increased IRA activity
1973	Northern Ireland Constitutional Act: makes it illegal for any public authority to discriminate on grounds of religious belief or political opinion
1973	Elections for Power-Sharing Assembly at Stormont: power-sharing fails
1980	'Anglo-Irish Intergovernmental Council': tacitly acknowledged by London that Dublin has a say in Northern Ireland affairs
1985	Anglo-Irish Agreement: opposed by most Ulster Unionists
1994	IRA and UVF Ceasefire Downing Street Declaration: Dublin and London to work together to achieve lasting peace in Northern Ireland
1996	IRA ends Ceasefire

The linguistic history of Ireland

Irish writers show a marked interest in – some might say obsession with – language, largely because of the major shift from Irish to English which occurred from the second half of the nineteenth century. The renowned Irish writer James Joyce (1882-1941) emphasised his awareness of the shift in *A Portrait of the Artist as a Young Man* (1914–15) when he had the chief character, Stephen Daedalus, describe his awareness that English did not mean the same to an Irish user as to an English one:

> He felt with a smart of dejection that the man to whom he was speaking was a countryman of Ben Jonson. He thought:
> – The language in which we are speaking is his before it is mine. How different are the words home, Christ, ale, master, on his lips and on mine! I cannot speak or write these words without unrest of spirit. His language, so familiar and so foreign, will always be for me an acquired speech. I have not made or accepted its words. My voice holds them at bay. My soul frets in the shadow of his language.
> (p. 189)

And the poet, Tom Paulin (*b.* 1949), has emphasised the struggles etched into the English language that is used in Ireland: '... the history of a language is often a story of possession and dispossession, territorial struggle and the establishment or imposition of a culture' (*A New Look at the Language Question, Ireland and the English Crisis*, Bloodaxe Press, Newcastle-upon-Tyne, 1984, p. 178). The obsession with language, especially in Catholic writers whose ancestors spoke Irish Gaelic, is the result of an internal conflict. There is love of and delight in the English language, the legacy of the conqueror, and there is a sense of loss and betrayal in the haste with which writers gave up their ancestral mother tongue. Brendan Behan (1923–64) was conscious of this duality when he said: 'Other people have a nationality. The Irish and the Jews have a psychosis.' (*Richard's Cork Leg*, Act 1)

Irish Gaelic

The original mother tongue of the Irish was Irish Gaelic, a Celtic language, closely related to Scots Gaelic and Manx, and more distantly related to Welsh and Breton. Ireland never seems to have been integrated into the Roman Empire although the Romans called the island Hibernia, a word related to the Latin *hibernus* 'winter'. Ireland's contact with Rome was mainly religious, rather than political or military, and the contact was particularly fruitful as far as literature was concerned. The Irish adopted a modified form of the Latin alphabet in the fifth century and the monks began to produce the first written vernacular literature in Europe north of the Alps. There is an unbroken tradition of Irish literature from that time to the present day.

It would be difficult to offer a comprehensive study of Irish Gaelic here but this language fundamentally affected Hiberno-English, the English of people whose ancestral mother tongue was Gaelic. Many Gaelic structures were carried over into the English of Irish speakers and many are used by Friel to suggest that his characters are Irish-speaking even though they use English.

The English language in Ireland

It is impossible to be absolutely precise about when the English language became dominant in Ireland. In 1600 the majority of people in the island spoke only Irish Gaelic but by 1900 fewer than 5 per cent of the population used Irish as their sole mother tongue. There were, as we have seen, two main waves of English settlement in Ireland: the first began in 1155 and the second began in the sixteenth century when the Tudors determined to reconquer Ireland.

There is little reliable linguistic information about the varieties of English spoken in Ireland before the seventeenth century. The Anglo-Norman conquerors of Ireland were ethnically mixed: there were Flemings, Normans and Welsh as well as English, and so although Norman French had high prestige, it is probable that English was the main language used among the invaders and between them and the Irish.

The English of the Anglo-Norman settlers and their descendants was called 'Yola' meaning 'old', because it seemed archaic to visitors from

England. Yola was superseded by the speech of the second wave of British who settled in Ireland during the sixteenth and seventeenth centuries, but traces of Yola survived in Wexford and Dublin until the nineteenth century.

The Tudors began the policy of planned settlements. Gradually, large numbers of English and Scottish 'planters' settled, and there were, for the first time in Ireland, communities of English speakers who preserved a separate identity from the native population, from whom they were marked out by language, religion and culture.

The Irish language at first withstood the incursions from Vikings, Anglo-Normans and Tudors. Many learned the tongue of the invaders, but gradually the invaders were absorbed into the community, adopting the local customs and language.

At the beginning of the seventeenth century, Irish was the most widely used language in the island, but within 300 years a language shift had occurred. The reasons for the shift have more to do with social conditions than with linguistic preference. Cromwell's settlements in the seventeenth century were

> . . . the most catastrophic land confiscation and social upheaval in Irish history, involving the expropriation of Catholic landowners . . . on a vast scale, the transplantation to Connacht of most of those who survived, and an influx of English landowners and settlers.
>
> T. W. Moody (Ulster Question, 1974, p. xliv)

The eighteenth-century Penal Laws reduced the native population to subsistence level, effectively further restricting the use of the Irish language so that, by 1800, Irish was no longer the first language for those people who had achieved any degree of economic success or for those who hoped to improve their political or social position.

A third factor contributing to the decline of Gaelic was the introduction of National Schools in 1831. In these English was the sole medium of instruction, so the schools hastened the language shift by their 'unrelenting determination to stamp out the Irish language' (Douglas Hyde, *The Literary History of Ireland*, 1899, pp. 631–2).

The final blow to the survival of Irish was the potato famine of 1846–9. No one is certain how many people died from starvation because the precise population was unknown. The historian, Cecil Woodham-Smith (in *The Great Hunger*, 1962, pp. 31 and 411) suggests that it might have been as high as 3 million or one third of the population. A more conservative estimate suggests that the series of famines cost 1.5 million lives, 1 million of them speakers of Irish; a further 1.5 million are thought to have emigrated.

The available statistics reinforce the points made above. The 1851 census estimated that about 1.5 million, or 23 per cent of the population, spoke Irish as their first language. The census of 1900 suggests that there were only 21,000 (approximately 5 per cent of the population) who spoke only Irish. This was probably an underestimate since Irish was, at the time, a language of low prestige but, whatever the true figure was, today there are perhaps as few as 100,000 Irish people speaking Irish as one of their mother tongues, and fewer than 50,000 use it as their main means of communication.

Hiberno-English

As well as varieties of planter English, there is also 'Hiberno-English' (H-E), spoken mainly by uneducated speakers whose ancestral mother tongue was Irish. This variety of language is strongest in the vicinity of the Gaelic-speaking areas, in rural areas and in parts of the country, such as the Sperrin Mountains in Tyrone, where pockets of Gaelic speakers survived until the 1960s. Hiberno-English is stylistically significant in the writings of dramatists such as Synge and Friel as well as in the prose and poetry of writers from communities which preserved Irish Gaelic into this century.

Friel does not try to recreate Hiberno-English in all its subtlety but indicates it by selecting a few features. (See Part 3, 'Commentary', p. 64.)

1. the use of words of Irish origin, such as 'Baile Beag' (Little Town), 'Bun na hAbhann' (Base of the River), 'Druim Dubh' (Black Ridge). (See p. 36 of the edition of *Translations* referred to in these Notes.)
2. the use of words of English origin but better known in Ireland than in England, such as the following from the stage instructions at the beginning of Act One:
   'hedge-school', 'byre' (cowshed) and 'a battle of hay' (bundle of hay)
3. the use of words and phrases associated with Hiberno-English speech, such as the following from the first four pages of Act One:
   'Wait till you hear this.'
   'Isn't she the tight one?'
   'And sure she can't get her fill of men.'
4. the use of spelling to indicate Hiberno-English pronunciation, such as these from the first pages of the play:
   'divil' (devil), 'yit' (yet), 'nivir' (never)

Irish influence can also be detected in grammar. In *Translations*, it may be found in the use of:

1. noun-centred expressions:
   'He's been on the batter since this morning' (p. 17) (= He's been out and about since morning.)
   'Put some order on things!' (p. 29) (= Tidy things up.)

2. foregrounding:
   'It's Irish he uses when he's travelling around scrounging votes.' (p. 25)
   (= He uses Irish when he travels around looking for votes.)
3. English prepositions in un-English constructions:
   'He's at the salmon' (p. 24) (= He's fishing for salmon.)
   'They're probably at the turf' (p. 24) (= They're probably cutting peat.)
4. reflexive pronouns for emphasis:
   'OWEN: And how's the old man himself?' (p. 26) (= How are you, father?)
   'JIMMY: Sure you know I have only Irish like yourself (p. 16) (= You know very well that I, like you, speak only Irish.)
5. present participles used in un-English ways:
   'And me taking it all down' (p. 16) (= while I was writing it.)
6. Irish-inspired metaphors, similes, idioms and proverbs:
   'That's the height of my Latin.' (p. 15) (= That's as much Latin as I know.)
   'You talk to me about getting married – with neither a roof over your head nor a sod of ground under your foot.' (p. 29) (= You talk about getting married when you own neither a house nor a piece of land.)
   'the big day' (p. 27) (= your wedding day)
   'a drop' (p. 30) (= a drink)
8. frequent references to God and religion:
   'Be God, that's my territory alright.' (p. 19); 'God love you'. (p. 22)

Friel, Steiner and translation

Friel read and was greatly impressed by the distinguished scholar George Steiner and his book *After Babel: Aspects of Language and Translation* (Oxford University Press, London, 1975). We can understand Friel's play and its preoccupations better if we look at some of the points Steiner was making. Among them are the following:

• Translation is something that we practise all the time: 'When we read or hear any language statement from the past, be it Leviticus or last year's best-seller, we translate' (p. 28).

• If we lose the ability to translate a dead language, then we run the risk of losing all the knowledge, wisdom and literature of an entire community: '. . . we can lose a civilization, if we forget how to translate . . . Each [dying language] takes with it a storehouse of consciousness' (p. 54).

• People often think that the languages of sophisticated people are more complex than the languages of peasants but this belief is not borne out by research: 'There appears to be no correlation between linguistic wealth and other resources of a community . . . Starving bands of Amazonian Indians may lavish on their condition more verb tenses than could Plato' (p. 55).

Many scholars have written about translation and, simplifying somewhat, we can say that there are two main views on the subject. The first is that all languages share deep-seated linguistic universals and so translation is always possible. We can translate English into Greek and Greek into Swahili and, indeed, Shakespeare and the Bible have been translated into hundreds of languages. The second, contrastive, view is that full, complete translation is never possible. What passes for translation, even between closely related languages, is merely an approximation.

Let us look, for example, at a few very obvious translations between English and French. The English word 'woman' can be translated into French as 'femme', but 'femme' can also be equivalent to English 'wife', yet, for a speaker of English, the implications of 'woman' and 'wife' are markedly different. The English sentence 'I love you' can be translated into French as both 'Je t'aime' and 'Je vous aime', but the first suggests an intimacy on the part of the speaker which English cannot exactly reproduce. In addition, the French sentences could also be given as a translation of 'I like you', but no English speaker would ever claim that 'I like you' is identical to 'I love you'.

Such examples should encourage us to think that, although a form of translation is always possible between languages, a perfect equivalent is rarely possible. Again, Steiner offers insights. As he puts it: 'The point is always the same: ash is no translation of fire' (p. 241).

Perhaps, as he suggests, only poets can translate truths and perhaps, also, the most intimate form of communication can be silence: 'In trying to build the tower [of Babel], the nations stumbled on the great secret: that true understanding is possible only when there is silence' (p. 286).

Ideas such as these underlie *Translations* and raise fundamental questions about how we look at life and reality. The American linguist, Benjamin Whorf (1897–1941), suggested that individual languages determine what we see in the world and how we think about it. According to this view, speakers of different languages do not merely inhabit the same universe and use different labels to name its parts; rather, we inhabit different universes if we speak different languages. Hugh suggests that language is part of the problem between the English and the Irish when he says: 'English, I suggested, couldn't really express us. And again to his [Captain Lancey] credit he acquiesced to my logic' (p. 25).

The title of the play

Friel's play is about language and language contact; and the problems of translating between languages acts as a metaphor for the problems of communication between the English and the Irish. Friel's preoccupation with language is clear from the title *Translations*, which is plural and which, in the context of the play, can suggest many things including:

- the expression of one language in another
- the expression of ideas in simpler, less technical terms
- interpretation
- the movement from one place to another
- the movement of sacred relics from one resting place to another
- the movement of a person from earth to heaven
- bringing someone into a state of spiritual or emotional ecstasy.

All of these 'interpretations' are useful in leading us to a fuller understanding of the play. As an illustration of the multi-layered meaning of the title, let me draw your attention to the cover.

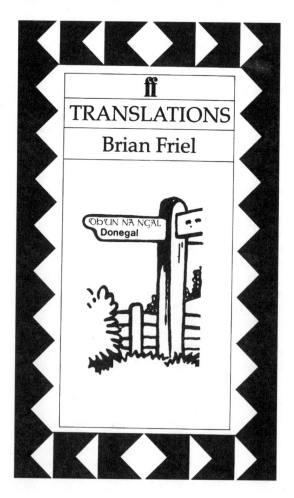

On it we have a signpost pointing west. On the signpost, we have two
names, one in Irish script, one in English. The English form, *Donegal*,
is merely a modified form of the Irish, *Dhún Na Ngál*, but the Irish
name means the Settlement of the Foreigner. The play is set in the heart
of Gaelic-speaking Ireland, and yet the name tells us that this is the
fortress or settlement of the foreigner. Lancey and Yolland are not the first
foreigners in the region.

The setting for *Translations*

The setting of the play is a hedge-school in a small town in Donegal called
Baile Beag (Ballybeg), but the theme is not similarly circumscribed. It
deals with cultural erosion under the pressure of an unsympathetic colonial
power, and the cultural loss that lies in the wake of the loss of a language.

The action takes place over a few days in August 1833, at the start of an
English cartographic mission. A detachment of British soldiers has estab-
lished a camp near Baile Beag and they plan to make a map of the area.
The translation of the local names into English and their recording in map
form may be seen as a metaphor for the substitution of English for Irish
Gaelic and the mapping of one culture onto another.

The problem of presenting two speech communities

In *Translations*, Friel presents two speech communities that are distinguished from each other in terms of language, nationality, education and
experience. In theory, the Irish community speaks Gaelic and we are
frequently reminded of this fact. At the beginning of Act 1, on pages
15–16, Jimmy and Máire talk about English:

JIMMY: English? I thought you had some English?
MÁIRE: Three words . . .
JIMMY: Sure you know I have only Irish like yourself.

and, just before the audience is introduced to Captain Lancey and
Lieutenant Yolland, Owen again reminds it:

OWEN: I'm employed as a part-time, underpaid, civilian interpreter. My
job is to translate the quaint, archaic tongue you people persist in
speaking into the King's good English. (p. 29)

In fact, of course, both Irish and English characters are represented by
means of dialogue in English. In the theatre, this linguistic device does not
pose much of a problem because the Irish and English characters are
distinguished by their accents, their names and their dress. In the written
medium, too, we are provided with clues that help to preserve the fiction

that two languages are being used. First, as we have seen, the Irish characters often remind us that they are speaking Gaelic. Secondly, the English characters comment on the problems of communication. On p. 30, for example, Captain Lancey asks: 'Do they speak *any* English, Roland?' and the interaction between Máire and Yolland (pp. 47–52) is peppered with comments to show that they do not understand each other's words. The third device to remind the reader of the linguistic split is in the language used by the Irish characters. The words are English but the idiom is different. We have expressions such as 'the height of my Latin' (p. 15) rather than 'the extent of my Latin', the frequent use of 'sure' as in 'sure seven nines are fifty-three' (p. 24) and the use of 'footless drunk' rather than 'legless' in 'you and I are going to get footless drunk' (p. 27).

A note on the text

The text used in these notes is the first edition of *Translations* published by Faber and Faber in London in 1981. Other texts are available but the page numbers may differ from those cited here.

Part 2

Summaries
of TRANSLATIONS

General summary of *Translations*

The play opens in a hedge-school that is run by a headmaster, Hugh Mór (Big) O'Donnell, who is fluent in Greek, Latin and English as well as his mother tongue, Irish Gaelic. The headmaster, who is as fond of drink as he is of poetry and philosophy, has not turned up in time for the evening class because he is attending a christening and is unwilling to leave the celebrations. The class is being run by Manus, Hugh's first son, and to begin with there are only two pupils, Sarah, who is thought to be dumb, and Jimmy, a man in his sixties, nicknamed the 'Infant Prodigy'.

Manus gently encourages Sarah to talk and, with his help, she begins to articulate her own name, while Jimmy reveals his intimate knowledge of Greek and Latin and his love of classical literature. Gradually, other characters appear. Máire is interested in learning English, which she sees as a means of escaping poverty. She would like to marry Manus but she needs to help her family financially and she realises that the only way to do so is by emigrating to America. An alternative would be if Manus applied for the headship of the new National School that is about to open. This new, free school will put an end to the hedge-school, and the salary of £56 a year would guarantee their security, but Manus, in spite of his promises to Máire, is unwilling to oppose his father, who has applied for the post already.

As other pupils arrive, we learn about recent events in the area: British soldiers have come to survey the locality and produce maps; the Donnelly twins have not been seen for some time although there are rumours that they have been harassing the British troops; and Bridget tells that there may be a potato blight in a neighbouring region because her brother had smelt 'the sweet smell' of rotting potato stalks.

The headmaster eventually arrives, intoxicated but not drunk. He has met Captain Lancey, the leader of the Royal Engineers, and has heard Lancey's complaints about the loss of horses and equipment. The pupils express a certain discontent that they spend their time learning Greek and Latin when English would be more useful to them. Máire, in particular, feels that English would help her if and when she has to emigrate to America to help support her brothers and sisters.

Hugh's second son, Owen, arrives. He has left Baile Beag six years earlier, to work in Dublin and, although he seems to have done reasonably well, he quashes the rumours of the fabulous wealth he has acquired. He has been hired as a translator to help Captain Lancey and Lieutenant Yolland to prepare a map of the region, as part of a major undertaking to produce a comprehensive survey of the entire country. Owen introduces Captain Lancey and Lieutenant Yolland to his family and friends in the hedge-school and underplays the potential seriousness of the cartography expedition by omitting to translate Captain Lancey's words accurately.

Yolland and Hugh are renaming all the places in the area for the new map but they are making slow progress, partly because Yolland has fallen in love with Ireland and will not be rushed and partly because they drink too much poteen. Manus arrives, very excited. He is delighted because he has been offered a job in Inis Meadhon which will give him the independence he needs to ask Máire to marry him. Yolland tries to be friendly although Manus keeps his distance, but they all have a drink to celebrate Manus's good news. Máire comes in to deliver milk and is a little angry that Manus has not told her his good news first. The attraction between her and Yolland is clear and she tells him about a dance the following night.

Yolland and Máire have left the dance and are running hand in hand. They try to communicate and, although they cannot speak each other's language, they can communicate their love. Sarah, however, has seen them leave the dance and runs to tell Manus.

Back in the hedge-school next day everyone is present except Yolland, who has disappeared, possibly kidnapped by the Donnelly twins; Manus, realising he has lost Máire, leaves Baile Beag for County Mayo; Lancey threatens the area with terrible retribution if Yolland is not returned; Sarah loses her ability to talk; Hugh is told that he will not get a post in the new school; Jimmy loses his ability to distinguish between the real world and the world of the Classics; and Máire, out of her mind with grief, returns to the school to wait for Yolland and to learn English.

Detailed summaries

Act One

The first act takes place over a few hours on an August afternoon in 1833. The scene is a hedge-school that is held in a disused barn. The hedge-school in Baile Beag teaches the basic skills but also the Classics. It does not, however, teach English.

In Act One we meet all the characters who will be of significance in the play and we become aware of the dangers that threaten this Gaelic stronghold, from within and without. We meet Hugh Mór O'Donnell, teacher, philosopher and drinker, and we meet his two sons, Manus, who is under the shadow of his father and Owen, who has escaped from the village but now returns as a translator for the British. We meet the pupils: Sarah, who needs to be coaxed to speak, Jimmy Jack Cassie, who lives in a world of virtual reality where the actions of Greek gods and goddesses mean more than the actions of those living in Baile Beag; Bridget and Doalty, who introduce news of the outside world, including the possible blight of the potato crop and the potential problems between soldiers and locals; and Máire, who would like to marry Manus but knows that Manus will never offer her security because he will never stand up to his father. We do not actually meet the Donnelly twins but they are mentioned and their absence is seen as threatening; and we meet the leaders of the English soldiers, Captain Lancey, who genuinely believes that his mapping mission will eventually improve the lives of all the people of Ireland, and Lieutenant Yolland, already in love with the country and the language and ready to fall in love with Máire.

Owen mentions several times that nothing has changed in the hedge-school: Jimmy continues to live in the world of the Classics; the pupils continue to learn Greek and Latin, rather than English; and Hugh continues to drink and to teach in his own way. The arrival of the soldiers does not cause but coincides with a period when changes are about to happen. The hedge-school is doomed because the new National School, where English will be the medium of education, is about to open; the hoped-for marriage between Máire and Manus will not take place because Máire will have to emigrate to America; and hovering over the village all the time is the twin worry of destruction by the potato blight or destruction by the British army.

NOTES AND GLOSSARY:
Page 11
The hedge-school: these were not uncommon in rural areas in Ireland before the introduction of National Schools in 1831. Before 1829, when Catholic Emancipation was granted, there were no arrangements for the education of Catholics in Ireland. Some educated Catholics established 'hedge-schools', often held in the evenings in barns, where Catholics who could afford to pay a little could learn to read, write and count. The education was conducted almost exclusively through the medium of Irish Gaelic

byre: cowshed. The reference to the disused byre where cows were once milked, suggests that the owners were once more prosperous than they are now. The O'Donnells seem to have fallen on hard times. The lack of affluence is reinforced by the stairway 'without a banister' and by the tools that are unused or broken, and by the adjective 'comfortless'

battle of hay: small bale of hay. The phrase is more frequently 'bottle of hay'

churn: large wooden vessel in which milk is turned into butter

slate: black writing tablet. The slate could be wiped and re-used. This is the origin of the expression 'to wipe the slate clean'

shabby: the clothes of all the local people are poor, suggesting hardship and poverty

lame: again a suggestion of poverty, certainly a lack of medical care

the Infant Prodigy: this is an ironic nickname for someone in his sixties but it also reveals that nothing has changed here since his childhood, that there is litte hope of advancement for a bright child. The nickname is also, possibly, a parody of 'the Infant Jesus'

Page 12
Ton . . . Athene: Jimmy is shown to read Classical Greek. The quotation comes from Homer's *Odyssey* and means 'but the flashing-eyed goddess Athena then answered him'. There is an ironic parallel between Sarah responding to Manus and Athena responding to Odysseus. The epic poem describes the ten-year journey of Odysseus (*Ulysses* in Latin) from the siege of Troy to his home in Ithaca; on the way he endures many tests at the hands of the gods but, because of his courage and ingenuity, he is eventually reunited with his wife, Penelope

My name is . . .: the reference to naming within the first seconds of the play and the difficulty Sarah experiences in saying her name are an early indication of one of the play's themes. Manus is perhaps the only person who gives Sarah the time and care that she needs. With coaxing and kindness she begins to articulate her name

Nobody's listening: this comment is both literal and subsequently significant. Jimmy is not listening to either Manus or Sarah just as other characters fail to listen to each other

alla . . . domois: 'but he sits at ease in the halls of the sons of Athens'. Jimmy is equally at home in the halls of Athens and in his local community

Now we're really started: Sarah can speak as long as she has help and support. She responds well to Manus and perhaps misinterprets the hugs that he gives her

Nothing'll stop us now!: an example of dramatic irony; the events of the next few days will stop Sarah speaking for good

Soon ... head of yours: the secrets that are locked in Sarah's head are like the secrets locked in a language. They can only be shared when sympathy and understanding are shown. Friel regularly provides the audience with reminders that the Irish characters are not speaking English by using structures based on Irish patterns such as 'in that head of yours' rather than the simpler 'in your head'

James: multiple naming is a feature of Irish communication. 'Jimmy' is usually called by this familiar form, but 'James' can be used to suggest a different mood. Here it is used partly to give deference to an older man and partly to express the pleasure that Manus is feeling (see pp. 63–4)

Maybe ... stools?: Would you set the stools out please? This polite request reflects Irish usage where a subjunctive structure indicates courtesy even in something as simple as asking Sarah to help to arrange the room for the class

Page 13

Wait ... this: the expression is normally the prelude to a piece of interesting news or gossip but to Jimmy the actions of the *Odyssey* are much more interesting than local news

I'll ... down: This is a Hiberno-English (H-E) construction meaning 'I'll be down in a moment'

Hos ara ...: Jimmy is meant to translate the Greek into Irish and the audience is reminded of this partly by means of his Hiberno-English (H-E) constructions. He uses two prepositions 'the flaxen hair *from off* his head' where Standard English requires only 'from' and he also uses a pronunciation found in H-E, *divil* for 'devil' and also, in other conversations, *nivir* for 'never' and *yit* for 'yet'. Later, on the same page, Jimmy uses two other Irishisms, 'sure' at the beginning of a sentence and 'myself' at the end. He associates his own unkempt appearance with the punishment meted out to Ulysses

Of course I would: Manus reinforces the impression that they are speaking Irish by not using 'yes'. He also panders to

Jimmy's daydream that his remaining grey locks could be similar to Ulysses' golden hair

Isn't she the tight one?: Isn't she mean? Jimmy uses the present tense for his description, emphasising his identification with the people and events described in the *Odyssey*. Manus, however, is less involved in the world of myths and legends and uses the past tense 'She was a goddess'

You couldn't watch her: this is an emphatic H-E way of saying 'She's unpredictable'

By God: when Jimmy gets excited, his speech becomes increasingly marked by Irish constructions, of which frequent references to God are a feature

about the house: at home

it's not ... thinking about: an example of H-E foregrounding. The sentence is the equivalent of 'If you had a woman like that at home your mind wouldn't be on mundane tasks like stripping turf', the unspoken thought being 'it would be on stripping her'

Better still: that's even better

our own Grania: Grania was the heroine of an Irish tale recorded in the sagas of Finn MacCool and the Fenians. The Fenian Cycle of sagas was recorded in Irish in Christian monasteries but the stories almost certainly pre-date Christianity. Grania was beautiful and loved Diarmuid but was loved in turn by Finn MacCool when he was an old man; she ran away with Diarmuid to escape Finn. Jimmy speaks of her as if she were a relative and still alive. In a way, the characters in the Irish myths and legends continue to exist as long as people remember the stories

a class of a goddess: immortal

And sure ... men: And she is sexually insatiable. Notice again the use of 'sure' as an emphasiser

if you ... choosing: if you could choose between. Jimmy prefers to use nouns to verbs

Athene: Athene was a virgin goddess of wisdom and prudent warfare. According to Greek myth, she was born fully armed, and sprang from the head of Zeus. She is also referred to as 'Pallas Athene'; her Roman counterpart was the goddess Minerva

Artemis: the daughter of Zeus, a virgin goddess of the hunt and the moon. She had a twin brother, Apollo. Her Roman counterpart was the goddess Diana

Helen of Troy: a human daughter of Zeus and Leda, queen of Sparta, Helen married the Spartan king, Menelaus, but was abducted by Paris of Troy, thus bringing about the Trojan War. Helen became a symbol of female beauty. The Elizabethan dramatist, Christopher Marlowe (1564–93), in *Faustus*, Act V, Scene 1, refers to her thus:

> Was this the face that launch'd a thousand ships
> And burnt the topless towers of Ilium [= Troy]?
> Sweet Helen, make me immortal with a kiss.

powerful-looking: extremely beautiful

parish: district. Jimmy thinks in local terms and transfers Greece to Baile Beag

would . . . should: Jimmy asks Manus which one he would take. Manus encourages Sarah to speak by inviting her to pick for him. Jimmy does not wait for either of them to answer

no harm to . . . : I don't wish to disparage . . . This is an Irish construction

Page 14

bull-straight: straight as a dart to the bull's-eye

them . . . eyes: those . . . eyes. Friel uses a dialectal construction to remind us again that Jimmy is not speaking English and that, in spite of his great learning, he is a poor peasant

would . . . jigged up: would certainly keep a man constantly on his toes (although 'jigged up' also has sexual connotations)

Jimmy Jack: Manus uses a different form of address to indicate a different mood. It is not uncommon in Ireland to have two Christian names, both of which are abbreviated. For example, Patrick Joseph often becomes 'Paddy Joe' or 'Michael Patrick' 'Mickie Pat'. The statement that Jimmy is dangerous is meant as a joke. We might, however, want to ask if living vicariously through literature does not pose certain dangers

boy: lad, son, mate. The use of 'boy' as a term of address is perfectly acceptable in H-E when the speaker is older than the man to whom he is speaking

he: Manus's father, Hugh Mór O'Donnell. It is not uncommon for the most important person to be referred to simply as 'he' or 'she'. Manus is worried because his father is late for class

mimes: (*stage direction*) Sarah has mimed so often in the past
                   that it is still easier for her to mime than to speak
to put . . . baby: to name a child. Manus also shows a preference for
                   constructions with nouns
Anna na mBreag: Anna of the Lies. Nicknaming was a regular feature
                   of Irish village life (see p. 64)
may take: must take. The 'may' in H-E usually has overtones
                   of obligation. 'You may pay this bill', for example,
                   means 'You have no alternative but to pay this bill'
substance: material possessions, wealth
Those are lovely: Sarah is clearly very fond of Manus: she tries to talk
                   to please him and she brings him flowers. Manus is
                   unaware of her affection or of the effect of his kiss on
                   the top of her head and so, inadvertently, he hurts her

Page 15
Máire . . . carrying a small can of milk: (*stage direction*) pupils in hedge-
                   schools often paid for their tuition by bringing food.
                   We have already seen Manus bring in bread and milk
                   (p. 13) as his meal, suggesting the poverty of the
                   family
Is this all's here?:   Are we the only ones here?
this evening: classes take place after the day's work has been done
How's Sarah?:   How are you, Sarah? The question is addressed to
                   Sarah, not Manus, as is clear from the fact that Sarah
                   responds. In H-E, it is not uncommon to speak to
                   someone in the third person: 'And how is the woman
                   of the house, this evening?' or even: 'How is your-
                   self?'
I . . . at the hay: I saw you haymaking in the fields
And how's . . . Cassie?:   once again, Máire uses the third person. She
                   gives him his full title, partly as a mark of respect and
                   partly to establish a light-hearted dialogue. There is
                   clearly some tension between Manus and Máire and
                   so Máire avoids the opportunity to have a private
                   conversation with Manus, and talks to Jimmy instead
Would I be safe?:   Will I be unmolested if I sit beside you? Máire knows
                   of Jimmy's fascination with Greek goddesses and
                   jokes about his treatment of women
No . . . Donegal: You couldn't be in safer hands. Jimmy's interest in
                   women does not go beyond words
The best . . . memory: before the Great Famine in 1845, Ireland had a
                   series of mild winters and warm summers, excel-
                   lent conditions for hay but also for potato blight.

Frequently, in Act 1, the audience is encouraged to think that change in this community is inevitable and that the changes will not, necessarily, be good. Máire's comment that she does not want to see another year like this is an example of dramatic irony. Neither she nor anyone else in the community will ever 'see another like it'

***Esne fatigata?*:** Jimmy switches easily from Greek to Latin and asks 'Are you tired?'

***Sum fatigatissima*:** I'm extremely tired

***Bene! Optime!*:** Good! Excellent! Jimmy is here playing the role of the teacher, encouraging a student. Several of the pupils enjoy taking on the role of the 'master', possibly to emphasise that Hugh Mór is not always there to play his own role

That's . . . Latin: That's the extent of my Latin. Máire suggests that she knows little Latin, although the Latin she uses is both appropriate and grammatically correct. She immediately adds that she knows no English and that English would be much more useful to her than Latin. She uses the expression 'have' English rather than 'know' or 'understand' English, using another H-E construction

Three words: virtually none. Máire, like the others, tends to under-value the knowledge that she has

spake: saying

What's this it was?: Now what was it?

In . . . maypoll: the saying she has learnt by heart is archaic. Even in 1833, 'besport' was old-fashioned and dancing around 'maypoles' was rare. The spelling *maypoll*, rather than 'maypole', may have been used to suggest that Máire does not know the meaning of what she is saying and does not know the difference between a 'pole' (post) and a 'poll' (head). Since this utterance is supposed to be the first example of English in the play, we may wonder about its significance. Dancing around a maypole is colourful and enjoyable but doomed to last for a short time only. Perhaps it is a metaphor for the last period of pleasure in Baile Beag

Maypole: Manus, in his role as teacher, corrects Máire's pronunciation but his correction is ignored

God . . . Mary: Irish people often preface stories, especially humorous stories, about a dead relative by an exclamation such as 'God have mercy on X but . . .'

Page 16

Sure ... yourself: Jimmy overlooks his knowledge of Greek and Latin. The use of several features of H-E, such as 'sure', 'have Irish', 'yourself', reminds the audience that he is meant to be speaking Irish Gaelic

Bo-som: Jimmy is like a young teenager in his fixation on women. The use of 'bosom' rather than 'breast' is meant to suggest that Jimmy is selecting a word from a language that he does not know. His unfamiliarity with English is emphasised when he says 'two powerful bosom' for 'two beautiful breasts'

Diana: Diana, the Roman goddess of hunting and chastity

You may ... know: It's typical of you that you know such a word. Máire teases Jimmy for his preoccupation with beautiful women and their anatomy

Is ... about?: Is there any water in here? Máire may be using her thirst as an excuse for a quiet word with Manus. Certainly, that's how he interprets it and he apologises for letting her down the previous evening

Doesn't matter: the clipped response from Máire suggests that his failure to turn up the previous evening did indeed matter

Biddy ... letter: Manus is perhaps too willing to be at the beck and call of others. The generosity he shows to others gets in the way of his relationship with Máire. It was not uncommon for people to be illiterate in the nineteenth century. Often, the teacher functioned also as a letter writer

Nova Scotia: the play has barely begun and yet we have had two indications of people who have had to emigrate, Máire's aunt Mary and Biddy Hanna's sister

I brought ... no good: I took the cow to the bull to be serviced but the mating was unsuccessful. This detail is meant to be funny but we might note how many people in the play are also single and unproductive

Big Ned Frank: one renowned for his sexual prowess. This is meant as a joke; if the bulls cannot succeed, then we'd better send for the village stud

The aul ... lame son of his: The drunken old schoolmaster and his lame son ... The construction used by Biddy Hanna is again meant to stress that she was dictating in Irish, not English. The information provided, however, is interesting because this is the second time we have been told of Hugh Mór's drinking

footering about: wasting their time

She did not!: Did she really?

And me ... down: while I was writing it down. The structure 'And + pronoun + present participle' is used in H-E to indicate that two actions occurred simultaneously: 'She came in and her dancing' = She was dancing when she came in

them new national schools: those new free national schools. The use of dialectal 'them schools' is a reminder of the speaker's background

Poll na gCaorach: Hole for the Sheep, Sheepgap. The name where the new English-medium school is to be opened is significant. The hole suggests that it is an escape route but the association with sheep, who are thought to be followers not leaders, suggests that the people who attend this school may escape but there is no certainty about where they are escaping to

Great ... man: It must be wonderful to be so busy! Máire's comments are still clipped and barbed, suggesting again that she has been hurt

Wasn't ... voice?: Your father sang very well last night, Sarah

near three o'clock: celebrations often went on until the early morning. Manus passed by at twelve but, as Máire makes clear, the celebrations went on much later than midnight. This suggests that Manus is offering an excuse, not an explanation, for his failure to turn up at the party the previous evening

No ... pieces: It's no wonder that we are all shattered

I ... hay: I can help you at the haymaking tomorrow. Haymaking or 'winning the hay' as it was called in Ireland was a time when women, children and men all worked together to turn, rake and stack the hay

That's ... reel: Máire changes the subject. She does not accept or reject his offer of help. The title of the dance is certainly appropriate

Page 17

If ... good: Manus ignores her change of subject stressing that, this time, he will turn up if the weather is good

Suit yourself: Do what you want. Máire is still upset with Manus

The ... tents: the English soldiers camped in the valley. This is the first reference to the presence of English soldiers, and it is positive: they are coming to help with the work

I . . . me: We don't understand each other. Máire asks if this inability to communicate matters. Events will show that their failure to communicate does, indeed, matter

crabbed: angry. Once again, Manus refuses to be sidetracked when Máire changes the subject. He recognises, however, that she is angry with him

***Doalty . . . pole*:**   Doalty arrives carrying a surveyor's pole. Such a pole would only belong to the English mapping the area, and must have been stolen. There is the seed here of future conflict. Local people have carried off property that belongs to the English, property that is of no use to them but the loss of which could cause serious inconvenience to the English

Vesperal . . . all: Good evening. Doalty also imitates the schoolmaster's style. The use of 'vesperal salutations' instead of 'Good evening' is an example of elegant variation, using a higher style than the situation calls for. It also helps to reinforce the impression that the language being used by these people is not ordinary (and also that the teaching being offered has little practical value)

He's . . . pig: the schoolmaster is coming down past the King's Rock and he has had a great deal to drink. Bridget uses 'as full as a pig' which, in H-E, suggests that he has drunk too much but is not yet 'drunk'. If he were drunk, he would have been described as being 'as full as a shuch'

***Ignari . . . rustici*:**   Ignorant people, fools, rural people. Doalty continues to imitate the schoolmaster, using Latin for the purpose of insulting his fellow pupils. There is, also, an unconscious echo here of Mark Antony's speech 'Friends, Romans, countrymen, lend me your ears' from Shakespeare's *Julius Caesar*. Doalty, like many Irish people, enjoys playing with language. His 'translation' is not meant to be literal and the pairing of 'semi-literates and illegitimates' is done mainly for the sake of rhyme. Friel was also possibly thinking of James Joyce and such addresses as: 'Gentes and laitymen, fullstoppers and semicolonials, hybreds and lubberds!' (*Finnegans Wake*, 1975, p. 152)

on the batter: out and about. The word 'batter' comes from the Irish word bóthar meaning 'road'

wee ones: young children. Hugh Mór teaches the children in the morning and the adults in the evening. He sent

	the children home because he wanted to go out drinking
Three questions:	Doalty mimics the schoolmaster's habit of asking questions or giving answers in three parts. Usually, Hugh Mór does not get as far as the third part. The use of threes is well known in rhetoric, from Julius Caesar's *Veni, vidi, vici* ('I came, I saw, I conquered') to the Hollywood film *The good, the bad and the ugly*. Triads (groups of threes) have been popular in Irish literature for over a thousand years. An example is: 'There are three slender things that support the world: the milk from a cow, the blade of the corn and the thread in the hands of a woman.'
Responde:	Reply
Question C:	Bridget's question provides another reference to the schoolmaster's drinking
weapon:	big stick. The surveyor's pole would not mean much to anyone other than a surveyor
He'll . . . arrested:	Bridget's comment is an indirect explanation that Doalty stole the pole
Up in the bog:	Doalty uses foregrounding here, telling us 'where' before giving us details of who did what. People in rural areas dug their winter supply of peat from the bogs in the summer
her aul fella:	her father
Red Coats:	British soldiers
Cnoc na Mona:	Hill of Turf
Theodolite:	a surveying instrument for measuring horizontal and vertical angles; it consists of a small moveable telescope mounted on a tripod
byre:	cowshed. This is the second time that Máire reveals that her family is on reasonably good terms with the soldiers
etymology:	origin of a word. All of the pupils ask Manus questions and this is the first time that he does not know the answer. The word 'theodolite' comes from Late Latin but its exact origins are unknown, even to the compilers of the *Oxford English Dictionary*
yoke:	thingummy. In H-E, 'yoke' is frequently used as a general term when the particular word is not known. It can be used of a person or a thing
Will . . . up:	Doalty is being rude to Jimmy but there are two other things to notice. First, he couches his rudeness as

a request 'Will you shut up' and not 'Shut up'. Secondly, he is worried that his theft will become known and so he wants everyone to drop the subject. Jimmy is so unworldly that he thinks only of the possible etymology of the word rather than of the possible trouble Doalty could get into for stealing

you aul eejit you: this phrase is typical of H-E in its pronunciation of 'aul' for 'old' and 'eejit' for 'idiot' and also in the repetition of the pronoun. To call someone an 'aul eejit' is much less insulting than to call someone an 'idiot' or a 'fool'. It is often close in meaning to the English 'Don't be silly!'

Anyway . . . side: Doalty's action of moving the surveyor's pole twenty or thirty metres was meant as a prank but would be extremely irritating to the surveyors. It is similar to another practical joke often practised in rural parts of Ireland: turning a signpost to face the wrong way and so confusing outsiders

Page 18
Cripes: a modification of 'Christ'
Wait till you hear: this is used to preface something very interesting. It is clear that Bridget knows a lot more about Doalty's activities than the others do

They . . . apart: the surveyors knew that there was something wrong with their calculations and assumed that the theodolite was to blame. This confusion was a source of considerable amusement to Bridget

That . . . work: Máire thinks it is a childish prank and says so. Her comment, which seems to be complimentary, is intended to be ironic

a gesture: Manus attempts to explain Doalty's action. He was an irritant to the English soldiers. Máire is unimpressed by both the action and the explanation

arrested: Bridget is aware that Doalty is courting trouble and that such behaviour will be punished if he is caught at it

shaft for your churn: thick stick which is moved up and down to turn the milk into butter. Doalty's question involves sexual innuendo

you dirty brute: Bridget recognises the implicit meaning and responds jokingly. Her choice of language shows that she is not offended. It is roughly the equivalent of 'You big pig!'

headline:	topic at the top of the slate. Common 'headlines' were 'Transcription', 'Corrections' or a topic for discussion such as 'The evil that men do lives after them'
Big Hughie:	this is another example of multiple naming. Bridget shows little respect for the schoolmaster, using a literal translation of Mór and a diminutive form of 'Hugh'
Nellie Ruadh:	Red-haired Nellie (see p. 64)
Our Seamus ...	**father:** My brother James says that she was going to name the child after its father. Bridget's comment reveals tht Nellie's baby is illegitimate, but an illegitimate baby was not unusual in rural communities or, indeed, regarded as much of a stigma. People did, however, enjoy working out who the father was
you donkey you:	you blockhead
bucks:	young men. Bridget's comment makes it clear that Nellie's child may have been fathered by any one of a number of young men
call it Jimmy:	this jokingly suggests that Jimmy Jack Cassie is the father, but Jimmy is only interested in mythical women
You're ... Doalty:	You're teasing us, Doalty
Jimmy ... you:	the implication here is that Nellie's father is searching for Jimmy so that Jimmy can be forced to do his duty and marry Nellie
Come ... Doalty:	That's enough, Doalty. Máire has teased Jimmy herself, but she thinks that Doalty is going too far

Page 19

He ... heart:	Doalty changes the subject and pretends that Nellie's father has heard of Jimmy's classical knowledge
... and ... him:	Doalty continues to tease Jimmy, suggesting that Nellie's father would want to hear him reciting Horace's *Satires*. Horace is an anglicisation of the Latin poet Quintus Horatius Flaccus (65–8BC) who was renowned for his lyrics and satires
Virgil's *Georgics*:	Jimmy does not realise that Doalty has been teasing him and assumes that everyone is as interested in the Classics as he is. Virgil is the English form of the Roman poet, Publius Vergilius Maro (70–19BC). Between 37BC and 30BC, he wrote the *Georgics*, four books on the art of farming

Be ... territory: Doalty is not at all interested in Virgil but continues to tease Jimmy by pretending that he is

You ... you: Bridget reprimands Doalty but enjoys his banter. She is more interested in her appearance than in learning

Slow bullocks: Doalty mocks Jimmy by picking out the part of the translation that could have no relevance to him and his farming methods, but Jimmy is so engrossed in Virgil that he does not notice the mockery

corn, not spuds: corn, not potatoes. One of the reasons why the Great Famine was so catastrophic was because most of the land was given over to potatoes and when this crop was blighted there was nothing else to take its place. Jimmy's advice would have been a life saver, if it had been taken

Would ... fella!: Doalty finally loses patience with Jimmy who is, according to Doalty, too lazy to work but has no inhibitions about telling those who do work how the work should be done

Would ... yourself: this H-E expression means 'Have some sense!'

... alright. Let's settle down: although the spelling should be 'All right', this is the form that Friel uses throughout the play. Manus tries to re-establish order when Doalty turns his attentions and his sexual innuendoes towards Sarah

Sean Beag: Little John

at the salmon: fishing for salmon

Donnelly twins: the Donnelly twins are mentioned several times in the play. Their actions are basic to the development of the story, although they never appear on stage. Doalty seems to know more about the twins than he is willing to say

Page 20

How ... know?: Doalty answers one question with another. He does not, in fact, say that he is unaware of their whereabouts

Our ... and ...: Bridget associates the killing of the soldiers' horses with the twins. She knows more than she says, but worries that she has said too much and so changes the subject

Machaire Buidhe: Yellow Plain

It's easier ... it: the topic set for Bridget is significant in the light of the imminent loss of the Irish language with all its cultural associations

a dose:	this H-E expression has many meanings, none of them complimentary. Here it is the equivalent of 'puke', 'irritant'
ate me:	be very angry and scold me
It's very good:	Manus teaches by commending and reinforcing skills that have already been acquired
passage money:	many Irish emigrants were sent their fare on condition that they worked for their employers for a certain period of time. Often, they were treated like slaves, but since few Irish people could afford their own fares, they had no alternative
Because . . . since:	Máire could not have told Manus about her passage money because she had not seen him over the weekend. Clearly, Máire would prefer to stay in Ireland
There's . . . house:	There are ten children in the house, all younger than me and all needing to be provided for and there is no man to bring in a wage. The H-E construction 'and no man in the house' probably means that Maire's father is dead. It could also mean that he has emigrated and is no longer providing for his large family
What . . . suggest?:	Máire turns to Manus for help and advice but he turns the question back to her, suggesting that he is unwilling to accept responsibility
Did . . . school?:	Máire asks if Manus has applied for the post of schoolmaster in the new school. If Manus got such a job, their financial problems would be solved and Máire would not have to emigrate. In Irish society, it would have been assumed that Máire's husband would have shouldered the burden of Máire's responsibilities
No:	Manus's monosyllabic answer is most unusual in H-E and emphasises his negation of a secure future for Maire and himself
might:	Máire has assumed that Manus would apply for the job but his answer suggests that he only promised that he *might* apply for it
When . . . hedge-school:	Máire states the obvious. The hedge-school is doomed. If Manus does not apply for the new post, even his current standard of living will be taken away

Page 21

It's £56:	£56 a year plus free accommodation was a good salary in 1831. In 1931, for example, the average

annual earnings of a working-class man were under £90

My ... for it: Manus will not go in for a job in competition with his father. His loyalty to his father must, however, be weighed against his failure to strike out on his own or to support Máire

For ... never: Máire implies the obvious. Hugh Mór O'Donnell would not get the job because of his age and because of his reputation as one who has a drink problem

I couldn't ... him: Manus makes his position clear. He will not oppose his father. Máire understands the implication of his statement. She must fend for herself

Suit yourself: Do what you like. Manus's action does not really 'suit' either of them, but she knows it would be futile to argue and so she turns away, both literally and metaphorically, from Manus

Just ... smell: potato blight caused the flowers, stem and roots to rot, producing a sickly sweet smell. At this time, virtually the entire population of Irish people depended on a diet of potatoes. They were easy to grow, even in the poor soil of Donegal, and were both filling and sustaining. A blight on the potatoes could spread as quickly and as devastatingly as a plague of locusts and would result in famine

It ... head: I forgot

snakes in: this could be 'sneaks in', bearing in mind that words such as 'tea' are often pronounced 'tay'. It could also mean that the blight gradually destroys the plant the way a snake can coil round a victim, choking it

Sweet smell: Máire is a pragmatist. As she says, people regularly report the smell but it has never, so far, affected Baile Beag (Little Town). In a way, both the pessimists and the optimists had a case: the potato blight had occurred, in small pockets, in most years of the nineteenth century but, until 1845, the weather conditions had prevented a mass outbreak of it

The rents ... ever: at this time, the majority of the Irish lived at subsistence level. They paid rent, through middlemen, to absentee landlords for their smallholdings. They had no security of tenure and could be evicted for failing to pay their rent. Their diet was very simple. If anything happened to either the potatoes or the fish stocks, then they were doomed. The fears of the people were thus understandable

Colmcille:	the Dove of the Church. Irish saints were often reputed to have prophesied about the future of Ireland. St Patrick, for example, prophesied that Ireland would never be destroyed by fire, like the rest of the world. Rather, it would sink beneath the sea seven years before the end of the world

Page 22

lug:	ear. In parts of Donegal, the adjective *beag*, meaning 'small' is pronounced 'bug' and so is a perfect rhyme for 'lug'
g'way ... son:	Get back to the world of Greece where you are really most at home. The use of 'son' from a young man is partly explained by Jimmy's nickname, 'The Infant Prodigy'. His neighbours probably feel that he has never grown up, never accepted adult responsibilities
seven fives are forty-nine:	Doalty, like others at the time, learnt his tables by rote. He gives the answer for 'seven sevens', not 'seven fives'
You ... apply:	Máire's suggestion that Doalty apply for the post in the new school is not meant to be taken seriously as he is a bit of a 'dolt' in the classroom. She means to annoy Manus and to suggest that even Doalty would have a better chance of the job than Manus's father
at the age of six:	education was not compulsory at the time but the children who attended would start early, at the age of six, and attend the school for six years. In the nineteenth and twentieth century, many started work in factories at the age of twelve
And every child ...	Bridget describes the system that later became law when compulsory education was introduced for all children
nobody's ... law:	there was considerable opposition to National Schools, especially in rural areas where children's labour on the land was essential to the family's well-being. Eventually, however, the National Schools did, indeed, 'take on' and hedge-schools disappeared
You pay for nothing:	the hedge-schools were not expensive but the teachers in them had to charge their pupils. Those who had no money were often allowed to give potatoes, meat, milk or turf instead. Teachers in the National Schools were paid by the government
And ... spoken:	the National Schools did, indeed, use English as

	the medium of instruction and contributed to the displacement of Irish
cute:	smart, intelligent
Buncrana:	a town in Donegal. Townspeople learnt English earlier than rural people and so were thought to be smarter
yella meal:	the equivalent is 'mincemeat'. 'Yellow meal' was very fine and used to make a type of porridge
chalk:	pupils wrote on slates with chalk. All the pupils are frightened of the schoolmaster and want to appear busy when he arrives
jouk:	sneak
table-book:	a book in which the multiplication tables are printed

Page 23

wrecked:	exhausted
*gooses***:**	(*stage direction*) pinches her bottom
I'm ... you:	I like you very much
bugger:	so-and-so; 'bugger' here has nothing to do with 'buggery'. In H-E and certain other dialects, it is not necessarily a term of strong abuse
hardly ... walk:	too drunk to be able to walk straight
*Adsum***:**	I am here. In schools where Latin was a medium of instruction, children answered the rollcall by saying 'Adsum' = 'Present'

in sobrietate perfecta: in perfect sobriety

Vesperal ... all:	Hugh Mór uses the greeting that Doalty used when he imitated the master (see p. 17)
Ave, **Hugh:**	Jimmy greets the teacher respectfully. 'Ave' is usually translated as 'Hail!' because it is the first word of the *Ave Maria* (Hail Mary). Jimmy is, in return, greeted formally as 'James'
Was it Eamon?:	Hugh knows that Bridget is trying to work out the name of the baby's father and so delays telling her for a while

*caerimonia nominationis***:** (*Latin*) ceremony of naming, baptism

libations:	drinks. A 'libation' was the pouring out of wine in honour of a deity

Page 24

Pliny Minor:	Pliny Minor or Plinius Caecilius Secundus (?AD62–?113) was the nephew of Pliny the Elder or Gaius Plinius Secundus. Pliny Minor was a Roman administrator and writer who was noted particularly for his letters

I suppose ... dipping: Doalty enjoys seeing how far he can go with Hugh although he addresses him respectfully as 'Master'. If *baptisterium* is a cold bath, then logically, the sheep who are put into a cold bath are 'baptised'.

the day Doalty: Hugh is sufficiently sober to turn Doalty's joke against him, saying that a sheep had indeed been baptised the day Doalty was named. Hugh then seizes on Doalty's weak point, his knowledge of the 'seven-times tables'

Sophocles: Sophocles (?494–406BC) was a Greek dramatist. Seven of his tragedies are extant, including *Oedipus at Colonus*

Doalty Dan Doalty: Hugh mocks Doalty by giving him a longer name, equivalent to Doalty Dan, son of Doalty'. Doalty had not, in fact, said that 'Ignorance is bliss' but Hugh mocks his ignorance by pretending to praise him

Tulach Alainn: Beautiful Height

Nora Dan ... complete: Hugh mocks someone who thinks that she does not have to return to school since she can write her name. Hugh's questions about absentees are not just duty: every pupil who leaves reduces his income

one and eight: 8.5 pence in today's currency

one and six: 7.5 pence

Gratias ... ago: I offer my thanks to you. Hugh seems to prefer Latin when addressing his pupils

studia: studies

three ... you: Doalty's earlier imitation of the schoolmaster highlighted his tendency to use triads

a bowl ... black: Hugh treats his son as if he were a servant. He does not even show him respect by using his name or saying 'please' or 'thank you'

perambulations: walk

Perambulare: Máire has said earlier that she knows very little Latin, but such evidence as this suggests that she underestimates her abilities

Captain Lancey: the chief officer in charge of the Royal Engineers

two ... mislaid: this is a different perspective on the stolen property. It may seem like a joke to Doalty but Captain Lancey takes it very seriously

Page 25

commerce ... suited: English has become the language of trade so it is well suited to commerce

our own culture ... conjugation: our culture is more easily expressed in Latin and Greek than in English. One might remember that Latin and Greek record the glories of dead civilisations, suggesting perhaps that the culture expressed in Irish is also, perhaps, doomed

acquiesco: I agree. The Latin verb was normally learnt in four parts: *acquiesco* (I agree), *acquiescere* (to agree), *acquievi* (I agreed) and *acquietum* (agreed)

Procede: continue, carry on

Dan O'Connell: Daniel O'Connell (1775–1847) was an orator whose election to the British House of Commons in 1828 forced Parliament to grant Catholic Emancipation in 1829. (Before 1829, Catholics were not allowed to sit in Parliament.) O'Connell was called the Liberator. He travelled round the country, using English when he spoke at mass rallies. He believed that Irish Catholics should fight for their freedom within the law and should force the English to change unjust laws. He also felt that the Irish should learn English, as well as Irish, for their own advancement. Some people regarded him as a saviour of the Irish; others regarded him as a turncoat for his willingness to use the English language and English laws. His importance in Irish life is reflected in the naming of Dublin's main thoroughfare, 'O'Connell Street'

Ennis: a town in County Meath. In spite of Baile Beag being a remote village in Donegal, news from other parts of Ireland travelled to it quite quickly

It's ... votes: O'Connell used Irish when the people to whom he was speaking did not understand English. He asked people to vote for him, even though he could not legally stand for Parliament, since he was a Catholic. This they did in sufficiently large numbers to force the British Parliament to grant Catholic Emancipation

Does ... politician: Hugh does not approve of Daniel O'Connell and shows his disapproval of Máire's position by refusing to address her directly. His attitude to O'Connell is indicated by the use of 'little', an adjective that was both literally and metaphorically inappropriate since O'Connell was tall

I'm ... Master: Máire is willing to stand up to Hugh in a way that Manus isn't, and to argue her case when she feels it is right. She gives Hugh the courtesy of his title 'Master'

I want English: Máire, like many people who wanted to get on in life, knows that she needs English

Page 26
I'm going . . . saved: Máire makes it clear to all of them that she knows she will have to leave the district and that she will be leaving within a few weeks
diverto: (*Latin*) I turn away
Mr George Alexander: the people in positions of power were English, as is indicated by the name
Mr Alexander . . . opens: it is probable that Hugh is lying about this. His qualifications are not in doubt but his age and character are against him. He covers his tracks well by insisting that he had told the Justice of the Peace that he would only accept the post if he could run the National School in his own way. That way, when he does not get the post, he can say that he refused to accept their terms. Mr Alexander would never have agreed to Hugh's terms. All National Schools had to be taught through the medium of English and had to follow a fixed 'national' curriculum
Euripides: Euripides (?480–406BC) was a Greek dramatist. Eighteen of his tragedies have survived, including *The Trojan Women*
Mr Alexander . . . run: it is unlikely that this is true. Hugh is ensuring that Máire knows that Manus will not get the new post and so will not be in a position to marry her
Owen Hugh: Owen, son of Hugh. Owen is courteous to everyone
Jacobe . . . agis: James, what are you doing? The use of Latin '*Jacobe*', the vocative of 'James', is another example of multiple naming
Máire Chatach: Curly-haired Máire. The fact that Owen comments that she is now a young woman indicates that he has been away for a considerable time. In fact, as he tells us (p. 27), he has been away for six years
the old man: the Patriarch. The expression, 'the old man' is not meant to be, in any way, disrespectful

Page 27
Fair: Hugh is not going to suggest that he is extremely well as this would mean he did not need the support of Manus
you . . . better: Owen knows how to manage his father
poteen: home-brewed whiskey pronounced 'potcheen'. Poteen was made from potatoes

footless drunk: legless, very drunk. Owen does not include Manus in his plans

nothing's changed: perhaps some things should have changed over a six-year period

the big day: the day of your wedding. People, usually children, were often teased by being asked if 'there was any word of the big day'. The fact that Jimmy was asked reinforces his 'Infant' nickname

Homer: the Greek poet who wrote the *Odyssey*. Owen's comment suggests that Jimmy was just as absorbed in the classics six years earlier and that his preoccupations have not changed

We ... Dublin: stories circulated in rural areas about how easy it was to make money in Dublin. It was like the view that the streets of London were paved with gold

taking ... at me: making fun of me. It is likely that the girls are serious, but the Irish tradition of 'taking a hand out of' someone means that Owen could not discount the possibility that they were teasing him

We left Dublin ...: the journey from Dublin to Baile Beag would be no more than 150 miles but transport was slower in 1831

Omagh: the main town in County Tyrone

Page 28

Get ... drink: once again Hugh orders Manus about. There is no suggestion of 'please' or 'thank you' or courteous request

We're ... day: Hugh's high-handed treatment of his pupils is indicated. He has barely started but is willing to end the class immediately

cartographer: map maker

toponymic: naming of places. Yolland's surname is an unusual one (see p. 63)

orthographer: one who studies spellings and writing systems

civilised: the original etymology of this word is 'city dweller' as all of them would know. Its other meaning of 'cultured, polite' is, in ways, also applicable

My ... Sarah: Sarah can respond to Owen's kindness, just as she has done to Manus's. Sarah gives her name as 'Sarah, daughter of Johnny Sally' or 'Sarah, daughter of Sally's Johnny'. The latter is possible because 'Sally' can be either a given name or a surname

Bun na hAbhann: the bottom/end of the river. Irish 'bottom' contrasts with English 'mouth' and Scots 'foot'

Page 29

Right ... Master: this is a variation on the theme of the well-known answer to one who is being officious, 'Yes, sir; certainly, sir; anything you say, sir'

You ... enlisted?: 'To take the king's shilling' or 'to enlist' was regarded almost as a form of treason by some Irish people. Manus is so absorbed in Owen's news that he ignores Sarah's achievement and, unintentionally, hurts her

Put ... things: tidy things up

Festinate: this command to 'hurry' is plural and so aimed at everyone

with ... foot: 'with neither your own house nor a piece of land on which to grow things'

you've nothing: Manus has no possessions, no prospects and no fiancée

Page 30

Gaudeo ... adesse: (*Latin*) I am glad to have you here. Hugh uses the 'I' form, stressing that he is the person in charge, the only one capable of welcoming them

What ... sir: Hugh offers Captain Lancey a drink, unaware that one should not drink while on duty

aqua vitae: (*Latin*) the water of life. The Irish name for whiskey is 'uisge beatha', literally, 'the water of life'

Roland: Owen is addressed as 'Roland', either because the English have not heard his name correctly or because they haven't bothered to learn it properly. The name 'Eoghan', pronounced 'Owen', occurs in Irish and is found in the county 'Tyrone', *Tír Eoghain* = Land of Owen

You may ... and: in spite of the fact that Owen has said he will translate, Captain Lancey speaks slowly and repetitively, as one might to a child who does not fully understand the language. This technique is often employed by people who are monolingual

Nonne ... loquitur?: Surely he speaks Latin? The use of '*nonne*' cannot easily be translated into English, but it is used when the expected answer is 'Yes'. In other words, Jimmy cannot believe that educated men would be unable to speak Latin

I ... sir: Captain Lancey's answer shows that he does not, in fact, speak Latin, because he has assumed that Jimmy was speaking Irish Gaelic. In spite of Jimmy's obvious poverty, however, Lancey treats him with respect, calling him 'sir'

Page 31

His Majesty's ... mile: Captain Lancey's work was part of a project to produce a detailed map of the entire country, showing water sources, hills, settlements, etc. Such a detailed map would make it very much easier for an army of occupation, if trouble ever broke out in the country

triangulation: a form of surveying in which an area is divided into right-angled triangles; the base and all three angles are measured, thus allowing the other sides to be calculated without having to measure them. The poles that Doalty has been moving are necessary for the measurement of the angles

six inches ... mile: just over 15 centimetres to the mile. This is a big scale and would have provided a great deal of information. If all the sections of the map were fitted together, its size would be in excess of 45 metres by 30 metres

A new ... country: Owen cuts out all the extraneous details in his translation, either because he feels they are unnecessary or, more likely, because the local people would worry if they knew exactly what was going on, assuming that the map would eventually result in higher taxation

This new ... law: Hugh deliberately mistranslates, suggesting the usefulness of the map to the local people rather than informing them about its actual purpose. Lancey tries to be as accurate as he can and he goes on to say that the map will, in fact, be in the interest of the 'proprietors and occupiers' of the land. The needs and interests of the proprietors come first

Page 32

George: Hugh and Yolland are quite friendly and Hugh refers to him by his first name. He does not indicate a similar degree of intimacy with Captain Lancey

Has he ... say?: Máire shows an interest in Yolland and in what he has to say. Owen fans Yolland's interest in Máire by suggesting that she longs to hear what he has to say

to rectify that: Yolland recognises the value of learning Irish and is very willing to take on this task

crude an intrusion: Yolland recognises that the map-making will interfere with the people's lives but apologises for any inconvenience they may suffer

Hibernophile: lover of Ireland and of Irish things

ramrod: a stiff, unyielding officer

'Uncertainty ... poetry': Hugh's appeal to a poetic authority is meant to excuse his mistranslation. His comment is like Robert Frost's claim that 'Poetry is what gets lost in translation'

military operation: Manus sees that the cartography expedition is, or could easily lead to, a military operation. It would be impossible for local people to hide from an army which had such a detailed map. Manus also asks the obvious question 'What's "incorrect" about the place-names we have here?' Obviously, there is nothing wrong with the names, but they are not English or understood by the English

Page 33

It's only a name. It's the same me: Owen is much less worried by changing names, assuming that a thing or a person is still the same, irrespective of the name used

It's ... Owen: Manus's comment is ambiguous. He could be agreeing with his brother but, more likely, he is saying that Owen is still the same as he was when he left. He does not share their strong feeling for the place or he would not have left it six years earlier

---

Act Two, Scene One

Act Two is divided into two scenes. In Scene One, we get to know Owen and Yolland. The survey mapping has already taken place and Yolland is attempting to take all the local names and to anglicise them. This can be done in two main ways: the items can be transliterated into an approximation of English so that Carraig Dubh becomes 'Carrigdoo' or they can be translated literally so that it becomes 'Black Rock'.

While Owen and Yolland are drinking and talking, they are joined by Hugh, who tells them about his plans for the new school and his new book. Yolland is impressed by Hugh's knowledge and linguistic skills but Owen thinks his father enjoys showing off.

Manus comes in to tell them that he has just been offered a job in charge of a hedge-school in Inis Meadhon. The job will give him the security he needs to propose to Máire. While Yolland and Owen are celebrating Manus's good fortune, Máire arrives. She seems less enthusiastic than we might have expected about Manus's improved prospects and invites Yolland to a dance the following night. It is clear that Máire and Yolland are attracted to each other.

NOTES AND GLOSSARY:
Page 34
creel: wicker basket
reference books: the books that may help in the naming process are the church registry, a list of freeholders' names and a grand jury list. Owen knows the Irish names because of his knowledge of the locality
that tiny little beach: this indicates the detail that will be shown in the map. If every little stream and beach is recorded, the map will be very precise indeed
Say ... again: Yolland is becoming intoxicated with both the poteen and the sound of the Irish language
Bun na hAbhann: this sounds like 'bun + nah + hoe + win' and means the bottom of the river. The English equivalent would be 'River Mouth'

Page 35
it's literally: this is not strictly true. The English and the Irish both use a metaphor from the body for the end of the river where it enters the sea. The English use 'mouth' and the Irish 'bottom'. Is this the same thing just differently expressed or do the speakers of these languages look on it differently?
Banowen: the names have been 'translated' before. This one little place has been given a variety of names. 'Banowen' is an attempt to write it as it is pronounced; 'Owenmore' is the equivalent of Big river'; 'Binhone' is a representation of an incorrect pronunciation
Burnfoot: this would be an approximation with 'burn' for 'river' and 'foot' for 'bottom'
We're ... enough: Owen recognises that they are not making sufficient progress and Yolland acknowledges that Lancey is annoyed with him because of this

Page 36
The sappers ... week: the work of surveying has been done and the engineering unit will be withdrawing within a few days
Can't ... English?: Owen is much more willing to co-operate with the English than his brother Manus is. Manus has already shown some understanding of Doalty's harassment of the troops when he calls it 'a gesture' (p. 18)
Druim Dubh: Black Ridge
Better ... without it: Manus knows that his father should not drink so

much and so he asks Owen to hide the bottle of poteen

your man: this particular man

Page 37

people ... me: Manus understands the stereotypical stiff Englishman, but cannot really come to terms with a man like Yolland

the Rolands: people like Owen, who are willing to give up their identity to the highest bidder

Father ... cradle: Hugh was responsible for the injury that lamed Manus, just as he is responsible for hurting his chances with Máire. The reference to Hugh falling across Manus's cradle suggests that Hugh has had a drinking problem for over twenty years at least

All he gets ... throws him: Owen is aware that Hugh's meanness will ensure that Manus cannot get married. Owen loves his father but recognises his weakness. Notice the verb that he uses. Hugh does not 'give' his son the money he earns; he 'throws' it to him

it'll ... suddenly: poteen is colourless, odourless and tasteless. Its effect is slow but strong. The uninitiated may drink too much, not realising how strong it is. Often, poteen is almost 100 per cent alcohol

Some ... resent us: Yolland is sensitive to atmospheres. He does not understand Irish but he understands that some of the local people do not like British soldiers

Dramduff ... Drimdoo: in some dialects the word for 'black' is pronounced 'doo'; in others, it is pronounced 'dove' to rhyme with 'above'. The different representations could have been caused by different pronunciations

The Donnelly twins: this is the third time they have been mentioned. No-one seems to know where they are, but if Lancey is looking for them, he must suspect their involvement in anti-English activities. All that we know about them is that they are excellent fishermen

Page 38

My ... addled: I'm confused

The ... lives: Yolland has been aware of Máire since they met in the classroom

catach: the adjective means 'curly-headed'. It is spelt *chatach* after 'Maire' because, in Irish, adjectives agree with the nouns they modify

Why . . . drop in: Owen suggests that Yolland should behave like a local and drop in to Máire's house when he is passing. Owen seems unaware of the danger to which he might be exposing Yolland

Poll na gCaorach: The Sheep Hole. The other names mean Little Town, Balor's Head (Balor was a king in ancient Ireland), Maol's Fort (or the Fort of the Servant), Yellow Plain, Foreigner's Town, King's Rock and Red Summit

Live . . . Buttermilk?: Yolland has fallen in love with the area but Owen tries to tell him that it would not seem so attractive if he had to live on the poor diet of the local people

You . . . here: Owen has been glad to escape from Baile Beag and tries to open Yolland's romantic eyes to the unromantic nature of surviving in such a place

Page 39

bucks: men. These are the men who offer Manus a job in Inis Meadhon

Loch an Iubhair: Lake of the Yew

capped: stopped

I was . . . the dew: Yolland, in his innocence, assumes that Doalty trimmed the grass around his tent out of kindness. It could also have been to mark Yolland's tent out from the others

East India Company: a trading company set up in London in 1600 to encourage trade between England and India and the East Indies. The company was dissolved in 1874. Often, second sons were sent to work in the East India Company

Tra Bhan: White Strand

Do . . . fate: Yolland does not immediately answer Owen's question. Fate might have been kinder to Yolland if he had gone to India

He . . . handwriting: Lancy may be stiff but he is a hard-working, efficient, painstaking officer. Yolland claims that Lancey resembles his father

Page 40

Waterloo: the Battle of Waterloo was fought in 1815 and was the decisive battle in the Napoleonic Wars. The English forces were led by Arthur Wellesley, the Duke of Wellington (1769–1852)

the very . . . fell: July 14. Yolland's father is thus 44. The storming of the Bastille was the start of the French Revolution

| | which aimed to establish a free, democratic society which would safeguard the ideals of 'Liberté, Egalité, Fraternité' (Liberty, Equality, Brotherhood) |
| **Apocalypse:** | an event of great significance ushering in a new beginning. In Christian terms, the Apocalypse is associated with the Second Coming of Christ at the end of the world |

I had a curious sensation: Yolland attempts to answer Owen's question about his belief in fate and struggles to express his feeling that, somehow, he was meant to live in Baile Beag

Apollo ... Ferdia: Apollo was a son of Zeus and the god of poetry, music, healing and prophecy; Cuchulain and Ferdia were heroes of Irish sagas; Paris was the prince of Troy who abducted Helen and brought about the Trojan War

I'd ... outsider: Yolland knows he would never be integrated into the tribe. Perhaps this point has been reinforced by the numerous references to 'Gall' in the names he is translating, where the word means 'foreigner, stranger, outsider'

hermetic: sealed so as to be airtight. Steiner, in *After Babel*, uses the same word in his discussion of language development: 'If we postulate ... that human speech matured principally through its hermetic and creative functions ...' (p. 231)

You can ... us: Owen suggests that Yolland could learn the language and the code.

Page 41

Quantumvis ... adest: Hugh's verse, translated in the text five lines below, might refer to the end of day or the end of life

Ovid: Publius Ovidius Naso (43BC–?AD17) was a Roman poet whose work includes poems on love and on his suffering in exile. Hugh's verse reminds one of the line quoted in Marlowe's *Doctor Faustus* 'O lente, lente, currite equi noctis' (O run slowly, slowly, horses of the night.) The line was quoted just before Mephistopheles came to claim Faustus's soul

***expeditio*:** an outing, expedition

to acquire ... literate: Hugh needs the reference to support his application for the post of schoolmaster. He is a snob but is willing to take a reference from someone he regards as his intellectual inferior

address ... circumspection: Be careful how much you drink. Hugh will never say something simply if he can use a Latinate variation. This was a characteristic Doalty seized on when he imitated Hugh in his absence (p. 17)

accommodation I ... require: Hugh's use of 'I' suggests that he thinks only of himself

journeyman: tradesman who was paid by the day. The word comes ultimately from French '*jour*', meaning 'day'

Wordsworth: William Wordsworth (1770–1850) was a Romantic poet who spent a lot of time in, and writing about, the Lake District. As a young man, Wordsworth was interested in the French Revolution, believing in its principles of justice and freedom for all. He would thus have had something in common with Yolland's father. Hugh's arrogance and insularity in assuming that Wordsworth would have heard of him are underlined here

Page 42

Roland's ... me: Hugh, like Owen, does not seem worried by the fact that Yolland does not know Owen's correct name

yourself and Jimmy Jack: there are many similarities between Hugh and Jimmy Jack, including age, background and classical interests

We ... posited: We like to think that we are surrounded by truths, irrespective of where the truths came from

Latin: Hugh prefers the Classical literatures and languages to his own, suggesting that he, too, may be contributing to the approaching death of Irish

it's ... ornate: the 'it' is ambiguous. Yolland may mean 'it' to refer to the Irish language or to Latin

A rich ... lives: the Irish language and the literature in it are elaborate. People who live in very poor surroundings often use languages which show great richness and ornateness

I suppose ... people: there has, however, been no evidence that Hugh or the others are 'spiritual'. Perhaps they are shown to be lacking in materialism but, so far, there has been no overt interest in or comment on spiritual matters. Owen certainly does not seem to agree with his father's interpretation

Greencastle ...: all the names, with the exception of 'Gort' have already been translated. 'Gort' means 'field'. Owen suggests that the new school is not at Poll na gCaorach as Manus said (p. 16) but at 'Sheep's rock', which would be 'Carraig na gCaorach'

Yes ... inevitabilities: Hugh ignores Owen's interruptions and continues to describe how the grammatical flexibility and ornateness of Irish may be a reaction against a life that is lived barely above subsistence level

Can ... half a crown: Will you lend me 12.5 pence? This was quite a lot of money in 1833, approximately one eighth of a teacher's salary for a week

I'm collecting: Hugh does not say from whom he is collecting or for whom his new book is intended. It is likely that he made the title up on the spur of the moment, possibly as a response to Yolland's interest in learning Irish

Pentaglot Preceptor: Five-language Teacher

the ... enterprise: Hugh confesses that the title is the best part of his book, possibly because it will never get beyond a title

Page 43

you don't ... calf: You don't dispose of the teacher because he has produced an excellent 'Teach Yourself' book. This association between a cow and a book refers to a famous judgement in Ireland. St Columba copied a bishop's bible and kept the copy for himself. The bishop claimed the copy and Columba appealed to the high king, who is said to have proclaimed 'To every cow belongs its calf and to every book its copy'

work of moment: important work

a civilisation ... fact: a civilisation can be trapped by a language which no longer represents life as it is currently lived

He's ... pompous: Owen does not deny that Hugh is astute but insists that he is vain

Is it astute ... survival: Is it smart not to be able to change with the times?

It's ... sorts: Yolland is not certain why the English are making a map of Ireland, but he thinks that it is a type of conquest that will result in people or languages being expelled

Something ... eroded: Yolland is more sensitive to the loss that change will inevitably bring

Tobair Vree: this comes from Tobair Bhriain, 'Brian's Well'; the 'Bh' is pronounced like 'v' and the 'n' ending was lost

Page 44

whose ... remembers: the sort of loss that Owen describes is common in languages. Was there ever a 'Hudder' who owned a field in 'Huddersfield'? If so, how can we ever know who he was? Stories are lost if people do not repeat them, just as a culture is lost if people forget their language

That's ... too: Yolland suggests that both he and Owen want to keep the name as a mark of respect to a man nobody else remembers

Page 45

A christening: Yolland and Owen are really naming the area and, in this way, they are taking part in a massive naming ceremony

Eden: Yolland renames Baile Beag, as a joke, but he does think of the place as being as perfect as the biblical Eden was

Lying Anna's poteen: it is debatable how much of the high spirits comes from their youth and how much from the poteen. Perhaps Anna's tendency to weave tall tales derives from her poteen

I'll decode you: I'll learn to understand and explain you

Page 46

I've been offered a job: Manus's job would mean he'd have to leave and go to Inis Meadhon (Middle Island) to start a hedge-school but he would have free accommodation plus a salary of £42 a year, certainly enough to get married on. Manus is not looking beyond the moment. Hedge-schools are doomed and it won't be long before a National School reaches the islands. The British are planning to map the island, too, in a few months' time

Where ... Anna?: Where is the poteen?

Next Monday: Manus will be leaving very soon

Page 47

I've ... Máire: Manus wants to tell Máire that they can get married and that she will not have to emigrate

There's ... back: Máire probably delivers the milk in partial payment for her education. She is quite abrupt with Manus, probably because he had shared the good news with others before telling her

Page 48

Fiddler O'Shea: Itinerant musicians were always welcome in a rural area

Tell him then: Máire wants Owen to tell Yolland about the dance, suggesting that she is interested in him

O ... sake: Owen does not want to be their intermediary

I want to talk to her: since there is no man in Máire's house, Manus plans to speak to her mother, presumably to ask permission to marry Máire. Máire realises this and deliberately holds him back

Act Two, Scene Two

Scene Two takes place the following night. Máire and Yolland leave the dance hand-in-hand. They struggle to express their feelings, knowing that neither understands more than a few words of the other's language. Eventually they kiss and are seen by Sarah who rushes off to tell Manus.

NOTES AND GLOSSARY:

Page 49

I could scarcely ...: although they do not understand each other's language, their comments show that they are in harmony

Manus'll ... got to: Máire realises that people will miss her if she is away from the dance for any length of time. Yolland, too, is aware that they might have been seen

The grass ... soaking: Máire deduces that the grass is wet because her feet are wet. Yolland thinks the other way and deduces that her feet must be wet because the grass is

Page 50

I've ... past: Yolland has noticed Máire since the day he arrived and has been watching her ever since. He does not say how long he has been watching her. It is only a few days but time has been moving differently for Yolland in this strange environment

***Tu es ... Britannico*:** You are an officer in the British army. Máire tries Latin as a means of communication

***et es ... agro*:** and are in the camp in the field

Water ...: Máire knows the words for three of the four elements: water, fire, earth and air

Page 51

your English is perfect: to Yolland, everything that Máire says or does is perfect

Norfolk: Yolland's mother comes from Norfolk. He clutches at anything that links them or allows them to communicate. The irony is that these meaningless words help to forge a connection between them

Mother of God: Máire worries that her aunt's piece of doggerel may be obscene

Bun na hAbhann: Máire can only recite English words her aunt taught her; Yolland can only recite placenames, but he recites them in Irish

Page 52

Loch . . . Buidhe: Máire joins him in a litany of placenames

I could tell you: they reveal that they have been watching each other

I would tell . . . : Yolland would tell her that he would like to stay with her in Baile Beag. Máire asks Yolland to take her away

---

Act Three

A further day has passed. Sarah and Owen are in the schoolroom pretending to work. Manus comes down from the living quarters with his possessions already packed. The atmosphere is very tense and, gradually, we discover why. Manus has decided to leave Baile Beag and go to Mayo where relatives of his mother live. Owen tries to persuade Manus to stay so that he will not be blamed for Yolland's disappearance. Owen tries to account for the disappearance by suggesting that Yolland has simply got drunk or gone off to visit one of the islands, but no-one seems to believe such explanations. Manus does not care about Lancey or the suspicions he may arouse. He had seen Yolland and Máire embracing the previous evening and had been tempted to hurt Yolland.

Bridget and Doalty come to the schoolroom but there will be no class because Manus has gone and Hugh has been drinking at the wake held for Nellie Ruadh's baby. It is clear that Bridget and Doalty know more about Yolland's disappearance than they admit. What Doalty does acknowledge is that the boat belonging to the Donnelly twins was on the beach when he went to the dance the previous evening but it had gone by the time he had taken Bridget home.

Máire comes to the hedge-school with an empty milk can. She is clearly distraught about Yolland's disappearance and knows that she was the last one to see him alive. They had tried to communicate: Yolland had drawn a map of England in the sand and shown her where he lived in Norfolk. They had parted with both of them laughing at the other's imperfect mastery of their language. Hugh tries to reassure her that Yolland is all right but the reassurance rings hollow.

Lancey comes to the school to make an announcement. He asks Owen to translate his stern warning: if Yolland does not return within twenty-four hours, all the livestock in the region will be killed; if he is not returned within forty-eight hours, then people in selected areas will be evicted and their homes destroyed. He asks Sarah her name but she is so frightened that she cannot say it any more. Owen promises her that her ability to talk will come back, but the promise is perhaps similar to his claim that Yolland will come back.

Doalty tells Owen that this sort of action had been taken before in his grandfather's time but that he was not going to stand by idly. Some people knew how to fight and he would join them.

Hugh and Jimmy return from the wake. They are very drunk and Jimmy seems to have lost his ability to distinguish between the real world and the world of the Classics when he tells Hugh that he and Pallas Athene are getting married at Christmas. Hugh contemplates the present and the past now that he has been officially told that he will not get a post in the new school. He remembers how he and Jimmy set off in 1798 to fight for Ireland's freedom, how they walked twenty-three miles in one day and then felt so lonely that they walked all the way home. Owen decides to go out and join Doalty, and Máire returns to the schoolroom where Yolland had been so happy. She wants to know what 'always' means because Yolland had promised to love her 'always'. She sits down with the two old men, waiting for Yolland to come back and Hugh promises to teach her English – tomorrow.

NOTES AND GLOSSARY:
Page 54
Murren: the English word 'murrain' means plague. The Irish placename echoes this but derives from 'Saint Muranus'. Even the saints are changed by the passage of time

Manus: Sarah uses her newfound skills to try to speak to Manus but he is too interested in his departure to notice

Page 55
You're not . . . army: Owen may stay behind when the army goes. It is even possible that he will take over Manus's role of looking after Hugh

Those . . . to go: Manus makes it clear that he is not going to Inis Meadhon and that he is not certain about where he is going or how long he will be away. He only knows that he must leave immediately

Clear . . . somehow: Owen warns Manus that if he leaves suddenly then Lancey will think he is 'involved'. At first, we are not told in what, but Owen soon makes it clear that Yolland has disappeared, although he tries to suggest that the disappearance may not be serious

I had ... him: Manus went looking for Yolland with vengeance in his heart. He wanted to kill Yolland for taking Máire away from him

But ... them: Manus had seen Yolland and Máire embracing and could not carry out his intention to kill or hurt Yolland. He could only yell at him ineffectually in Irish

'Sorry': Manus mimics the dialogue between Máire and Yolland. He does not actually say that he did not see Yolland after that

What ... islandmen: Manus feels he has nothing to say to Lancey but is anxious for his message to be given to the men from Inis Meadhon who offered him the job

Page 56

Mayo, maybe: Manus may make his way to County Mayo, perhaps seventy-five miles away, to a place where his mother had relatives

Tell father ... things: Manus takes two Latin and one Greek text with him. He had bought them with the money he got from selling his pet lamb. Manus had put books before the sentimentality of a pet. He also passes on the message that Hugh does not know how to look after himself or his money

two-and-six: 12.5 pence, but worth a great deal more at that time

press: cupboard

If Máire ...: Owen tries to find out what to say to Máire but Manus refuses even to mention her name

He'll ... soda bread: Manus shows by his comments that he has looked after his father's needs and has performed the sort of duties that would normally fall to a wife

Two shillings a day: Owen tries to give Manus money. He is paid by the day, like a 'journeyman' and, although 10 pence per day was good money, the work was uncertain and temporary

What is your name?: Manus encourages his pupil to speak before he leaves

you did no harm: Manus is referring to the fact that Sarah had told him about Yolland and Máire and is telling her that she is not to blame for Yolland's disappearance. Yet, ironically, by teaching her to speak, he gave her the means to destroy his life by telling him

Page 57
Where?: When Manus leaves, Sarah reverts to sign language
You're ... crack: You're missing all the fun and excitement. Doalty and Bridget bring the news that fifty soldiers have arrived and are combing the district
scattering animals ... And ... turf-stacks!: the soldiers are paying scant attention to animals or property in their minute search for Yolland
field of corn: the corn should have been harvested already but would be useless if trodden on by fifty pairs of boots
drawers: underpants
You hoors you!: this means 'You whores you' but in H-E the insult 'hoor' can be applied to either men or women
the wee get: the little bastard. Bridget and Doalty show little sympathy for Barney Petey's loss
Big Hughie: the schoolmaster, Hugh
the wake: celebration shortly after a death. This is the first reference we have to anyone's death

Page 58
Visigoths! ... Vandals!: three ruthless armies. The Visigoths sacked Rome in 410; the Huns came from Asia and invaded the Roman Empire in the fourth and fifth centuries; the Vandals raided Roman territories in the third and fourth centuries and devastated Gaul (France) between AD406 and 409
Ignari! ... Rustici!: Ignorant people! Fools! Country men! This is the same triad that Doalty uses on p. 17 to describe ignorant students
Thermopylae: a narrow pass between the mountains and the sea linking Locris and Thessaly. This was the scene of a famous battle in 480BC when the Spartan King Leonidas and 300 men tried to defend the pass and were wiped out by the invading Persian army
crack like it: Doalty and Bridget see this event as a great joke and do not consider the consequences of such actions
Big ... class: a reference to Hugh's stage of intoxication
What's on in Mayo: Doalty assumes that Manus must have gone to Mayo because something interesting was going on there. Owen has no qualms about telling Doalty and Bridget where Manus has gone
He left ... home: Doalty and Bridget must have followed Yolland and Máire if they saw them leave the dance and then saw Yolland take her home

We know nothing: Doalty is less willing to talk. He knows that, ultimately, it will be safer to 'know nothing'

If... twins: Bridget claims that she knows nothing about Yolland but that the Donelly twins might know. This is the third time the twins are mentioned. Their actions seem to affect the events of the play even though they are never seen

Hallowe'en: 31 October. Bridget changes the subject from Yolland's disappearance to the safer one of O'Shea's musical skills

Page 59

Didn't... were: Doalty does not want to be involved and insists he didn't see the twins

All I know ... Bridget: Doalty had seen the twins' boat when he was going to the dance and the boat had gone by the time he had taken Bridget home

I must... empty: Máire must try to behave normally but her action in carrying an empty milk can shows how upset she is

Sure... calf: Máire offers to go back for milk which will otherwise go to the calf and then reveals her real reason for the visit, her eagerness to know if they have heard any news about Yolland

I'll see you yesterday: Yolland's attempt at Irish resulted in his confusing the words for 'yesterday' and 'tomorrow'

Page 60

laughing: they were happy and laughing when they parted and now Máire wants to know if Owen thinks Yolland is safe

Winfarthing ... Norfolk: Yolland and Máire had been able to communicate in spite of the language barrier. He came from Norfolk

You were ... Boston: Máire compliments Sarah on her appearance the previous night when she wore a green dress that a relative had sent from America. Máire does not know that Sarah had probably dressed up for Manus or that she had told Manus about Yolland and Máire kissing

Brooklyn: Máire now realises that she will have to emigrate. She does not know that Brooklyn is part of a city and so she will never work in the hay again

Nellie Ruadh's baby died: the child whose christening Hugh had attended has died. Hugh and Jimmy Jack were attending the wake for him

It didn't last long: Máire is referring to the child but her summary could apply to her relationship with Yolland

Page 61

Bloody ... fool: Doalty realises that Manus will be blamed for Yolland's disappearance

beagles: hunting dogs that make a great deal of noise

They'll ... night: Manus's limp will slow him down and so he is likely to be captured before nightfall

This will suffice: Lancey decides to use the pupils in the school to pass on his message to the community at large

Page 62

Swinefort ... King's Head: Lancey uses the translations prepared by Yolland and Owen

Tell ... camp's on fire: Doalty has been looking out of the window almost since he and Bridget arrived, suggesting that he knew something was going to happen. In fact, he sees that the English camp has been set on fire

Page 63

I'll ... Doalty: Lancey promises to remember Doalty and even at a time like this he is courteous and uses 'Mr Doalty'. He also tells Owen that he must carry a share of the blame

our Seamus ... where: Seamus, like the Donnelly twins, never appears in the play but much of the information passed on by Bridget comes from her brother

The sweet smell: Bridget smells the tents burning but thinks it is the smell of the potato blight. The potato blight would have been an even greater misfortune than the loss of their animals and their homes

It will ... again: Owen tries to console Sarah that her ability to speak will return

When ... thing: the killings and evictions had happened before and all the efforts of naming places would now be wasted because the places would be destroyed

he'll not ... fight: Doalty is determined to fight even though he knows he will not win

Page 64

If they ... found: the Donnelly twins might be able to organise a fight and it is possible that Doalty knows where they are or how they can be contacted

***domus lugubris*:** the house of mourning. Hugh is telling Jimmy the story of what happened although Jimmy was there.

	Hugh assumes that the other pupils will be waiting for him
'My tidings . . .':	I have bad news for you
Manus!:	Hugh has lost all possibility of a job in the new school to someone who can cure bacon. Hugh does not realise that he has lost Manus as well as the job

Page 65

I'm going . . . married: Jimmy Jack has clearly lost his link with reality and announces that he and the goddess Pallas Athene are getting married at Christmas

Metis from Hellespont: Metis, wife of Jupiter, was devoured by him in her first month of pregnancy, lest she produce a child more cunning than himself. Pallas Athene (Minerva) sprang from Jupiter's head when it was opened up by Vulcan. But Jimmy is talking of her as though she were a local girl

Correct: Hugh humours Jimmy, who admits that all he really wants from a woman is companionship

Page 66

We must learn: Hugh realises that the new names will become the future names and that everyone will have to learn them

I know . . . live: Owen has found his identity as an Irishman. He suggests that he is not willing to learn new names. He does not say so, but it is likely that he will join Doalty in fighting

it is not . . . language: it is not the past that affects us but the reflection of the past that is transmitted to us via our language

***edictum imperatoris*:** the emperor's edict. Even at a time like this, Hugh translates into Latin

Page 67

To remember . . . madness: We would all go mad if we didn't learn to forget. This statement is almost an exact quotation from George Steiner's *After Babel* (p. 29): 'To remember everything is a condition of madness'

1798: Jimmy and Hugh had set out to fight in the 1798 rebellion. They were young men then, going to war with a copy of Virgil's epic in their pockets, i.e. full of poetic idealism

***my* goddess . . . :** in spite of his recent marriage to Dark-haired Kathleen daughter of Reactann, Hugh left home to fight against the English. He and Jimmy had walked twenty-three miles in a day and then had got home-sick and walked back home

desiderium nostrorum: longing for our own

pietas: piety, desire

I'm back again: Máire is wandering around uncertain of where she is going or what she is doing

When ... start: Máire is eager to learn English, more now for Yolland's sake than for its value in America

always: Máire had been told by Yolland that his affection was for 'always' but their 'always' lasted an even shorter time than Nellie Ruadh's baby

It's a silly word: Hugh is saying that nothing in life is permanent

Page 68

endogamein: (*Greek*) marry within the tribe. Máire and Yolland were not allowed to break the taboo of marrying outside the tribe

Part 3

Commentary

Background

The play will be interpreted differently by different readers. The response of an English audience may well vary from an Irish one, but one reaction is not necessarily less sensitive than another. A person who knows even a little Irish will, for example, respond to a name like Anna na mBreag in ways that would be unlikely for English speakers, even to those who know that the name means 'Anna of the Lies'. An Irish person associates 'bréag' with exaggeration, telling tall tales, rather than with untruths. In other words, the translation helps but does not, and cannot, explain the varied range of associations that we all carry to the words that we use.

Naming

The names of the characters in any piece of literature are significant. If, for example, we are introduced to a man called Mr Allworthy, we may assume that the writer intended us to expect the character to be upright and honourable or was giving an ironic title to him. Equally, placenames are often significant. If the action is located in Headlong Hall or Nightmare Abbey, for example, we might assume that the events are not meant to be taken literally. The names of characters and places in *Translations* are not so clearly marked as the ones we have listed above, but they warrant close attention.

Naming characters

There are only ten characters in *Translations*.

The Irish characters are presented to us by means of first names only; the two English characters are presented to us formally by means of their army title and surname. It seems clear that the audience is meant to identify more closely with the first-name characters than with the English officers. Even in the body of the play, when we learn Yolland's name, his speeches are signalled by YOLLAND, not by GEORGE, and the audience never learns Captain Lancey's first name.

In traditional Irish society, people did not have surnames. If Brian had a daughter called Máire and a son called Seán, they could be referred to as:

Máire Ní Bhriain (Mary daughter of Brian)
Seán Mac Bhriain (John son of Brian).
The English passed the Statutes of Kilkenny in 1366 and these
laws insisted on Irish people adopting English-style surnames. Many
people chose 'Mac' or 'O' prefixes to a first name, resulting in such forms
as McNeill, O Neill. 'O' was not an abbreviation of 'Of' but meant
'Descendant of'.

Each name in the play has a story to tell; three of them appear to be
Irish, namely Manus, Máire and Doalty. Yet Manus comes from Latin
'Magnus' meaning 'Big, Great' and also 'hand', perhaps suggesting that
he is Hugh's 'right-hand man'; Máire is the Irish equivalent of Maria.
'Doalty' is not a well-known Irish name; it is clearly meant to remind
an English-speaking audience of 'dolt' but it may also suggest 'Diúl-
tigh' (Doo+ill+ty) meaning 'I deny, oppose, refuse, renounce' to an Irish
one. This suggestion is reinforced by the fact that, at baptism, a child's
sponsor promises, on the child's behalf, to 'deny or renounce' Satan,
and by Hugh's comment (p. 24) that Doalty was appropriately named
at baptism. The other 'Irish' names are well known throughout Britain.
'Bridget' is from Swedish, meaning 'strength'; 'Sarah' derives ultimately
from Hebrew; 'Hugh' and 'Owen' are widely used in Wales and both parts
of 'Jimmy Jack' are well-known variants of 'James' and 'John'.

'Lancey' suggests 'lance' and may make an audience think of weapons
or an army. 'Yolland' is regarded as a blend of 'Old' + 'land' and may
remind some members of the audience that 'Yola' was the name given to
the form of English used by the first wave of English-speaking settlers.
These settlers gradually merged with the Irish, giving up Yola and adopting the Irish language and Irish customs.

Perhaps we should also draw attention to four other characters who play
a significant role in the play but who are never actually seen. These are
'the Donnelly twins', Nellie Ruadh and Mr George Alexander. The 'Donnelly twins' are named in all three acts. Their shadowy activities against
the soldiers are suggested in Act 1 and their probable abduction of Yolland
triggers off the destructive reprisals promised by Captain Lancey. The
christening of Nellie Ruadh's (Red-haired Nellie) baby is described in
Act 1 and its death in Act 3. The child's short life parallels the brief
period of understanding between the English and the Irish, as represented
by the love between Máire and Yolland. The last character, Mr George
Alexander, is referred to by Hugh in Acts 1 and 3. Hugh suggests in Act 1
that the Justice of the Peace, Mr Alexander, has offered him the post of
schoolmaster in the new National School. In Act 3, Mr Alexander tells
Hugh that the job has been given to Bartley Timlin, a teacher from Cork.
Cork was anglicised long before Donegal and so his selection reinforces
the notion that the English language will soon become dominant in the
region.

Nicknames and multiple names are also used in *Translations*, and such usage gives an Irish aura to names that are otherwise not, obviously, Irish. Because many people in Irish villages had the same surname, nicknames were common and fell into three main categories:

i those relating to the colour or condition of the hair, for instance Máire Chatach (Curly-haired Mary) and Nellie Ruadh (Red-haired Nellie)

ii those relating to size, for instance Hugh Mór (Big Hugh)

iii those relating to specific incidents or tendencies, for instance Anna na mBreag (Anna of the Lies) and the 'Infant Prodigy'. This last one illustrates another feature of Irish nicknaming: it often uses a joking term that is totally inappropriate such as 'Infant' for a man in his sixties or 'Bushy-headed' for someone who is bald.

Multiple naming was and is a means of indicating different attitudes, degrees of intimacy or seriousness in Irish society. Jimmy, for example, is called 'Jimmy', 'Jimmy Jack', 'Jimmy Jack Cassie', 'James', 'Jacob' and the 'Infant Prodigy', and each of the names stresses a contrasting attitude on the part of the speaker to the character. Often, a child may be christened 'James' or 'Jacobus' in Latin and called 'Jimmy' as a child, 'Jim' as a mature person and 'James' as an older man, but all three names, plus 'Seamus' and perhaps 'Jamesie', can be used to express different degrees of intimacy or humour or seriousness. The implications of multiple naming in *Translations* are suggested in individual notes.

Naming places

The entire play deals with naming places and the virtual impossibility of translating them appropriately. Let us concentrate on just two in order to illustrate this point. Most of the action takes place in a hedge-school in 'Baile Beag' or 'Ballybeg'. This seems to be a very simple approximation, but is it? In Irish, 'baile' means 'home', 'clan settlement' and 'beag' means 'little'. This name may suggest insularity but it also implies intimacy. 'Bally' and 'beg' have very different implications in English. 'Bally', if it is used at all, may be associated with 'ballyhoo' and 'beg' suggests 'asking for charity'. The second name that we might think about is 'Bun na hAbhann', 'the bottom of the river', which Owen decides to translate as 'Burnfoot' (River + foot) and which earlier translators called 'Banowen', 'Owenmore' and 'Binowen'. One of the issues raised by naming is most succinctly expressed in Shakespeare's question 'What's in a name?' (*Romeo and Juliet*, Act 2, Scene 2). Clearly, there is a great deal in a name in terms of implication and association.

Structure

Translations is divided into three acts and the events are played out in less than a week at the end of a hot August in 1833. Act One takes place in a hedge-school and introduces us to all the characters, first the Irish villagers, and then the English officers. This is the longest act in what is a surprisingly short play. Act Two is divided into two scenes, both showing efforts to translate and communicate. Yolland and Owen make slow progress with the anglicisation of Irish words because Yolland realises that their task is equivalent to translating a culture and a history rather than merely to translating words. The second scene is the only one in the play to take place outside the hedge-school. Máire and Yolland can hardly understand a word of one another's language but they can communicate their love to each other. The third act is full of possibilities, none of them good. Virtually everyone has lost something: Manus has lost the woman he wants to marry; Sarah has lost her recently-acquired ability to talk; Hugh has lost his livelihood and perhaps both sons; Máire has lost Yolland, her hopes and perhaps her mind; Yolland has lost his life; Jimmy Jack has lost his grip on reality; Nellie Ruadh has lost her baby; the area is about to be devastated as crops, animals and people face the anger of the army. Life in Ballybeg will be changed utterly. Perhaps, in the words of W. B. Yeats's poem 'Easter, 1916', a 'terrible beauty' will be born.

Most of the action takes place in the evening and in the hedge-school. There is no time for thought or wise counsel as the characters rush towards destruction. The acts get shorter, symbolising the speed with which the locals move from a timeless, seemingly unchanging society to a disaster which will change their lives, their language and their culture forever. The play ends with Hugh translating from the *Aeneid*, a possible reminder to the audience that all empires and cultures eventually fade, but their shadow can be called up if we remember how to translate.

The Irish and English characters are meant to speak different languages, but Friel uses the dramatic convention of employing English for both. The language is modified in structure to suggest differences between the nationalities and their preoccupations are shown to be different. The English are monolingual and monocultural, the Irish multilingual and, in this play, strongly attracted to the cultures of Greece and Rome.

The structure of *Translations* can be represented as follows:

The play: 57 pages and about 13,000 words of dialogue. When we remember that a radio announcer speaks about 200 words a minute, we realise that the play could be read in about an hour. Actions and breaks between acts lengthen this, of course.

Act One: 23 pages and about 5,500 words. This is the longest act. It introduces the characters and the two developments that are going to change the lives of everyone: the opening of the new school and the work of the army's survey team.

Act Two: 20 pages and about 4,500 words. This act is divided into two scenes and the dialogue indicates that a few days have passed. Scene One concentrates on Yolland and Owen. Scene Two concentrates on Yolland and Máire.

Act Three: 15 pages and about 3,000 words. The action takes place the evening after Scene Two. The play ends, as it began, with two men and a woman in the hedge-school. However, whereas Act One began with the hope that a young woman would learn to speak, Act Three ends with a young woman and two old men who have lost touch with reality.

Characters

There are three sets of characters in *Translations*: the Irish characters that we meet in the hedge-school, the two English characters who will change the lives of the people of Baile Beag forever, and the characters who are only named but who trigger off the destruction.

Manus

Manus is described as lightly built, intense and in his late twenties or early thirties (p. 11). Hugh, however, describes how he left his infant son in 1798 (p. 67) and this would make Manus thirty-five. Whatever his exact age (and Friel does not seem to worry unduly about precision of this kind) he is a mature man. Like the majority of the characters, however, he is single and has no children. The lack of young children is perhaps the playwright's way of indicating the sterility of the region.

Manus is an excellent teacher, encouraging Sarah to speak and answering all the queries put to him by the pupils. He is dominated by his father, allowing Hugh to treat him with a total lack of respect, demanding 'a bowl of tea' (p. 24) for himself and food and drink for their visitor (p. 28).

Manus knows that his only opportunity to break from his father, establish his independence and marry Máire is to apply for the post in the new National School but he will not apply for it even though he believes that his father will fail to get it. He insists that he cannot apply for the new post because: 'My father has applied for it . . .' and it would be wrong for a son to go in for a job competing with his father (p. 21).

Yet Manus's actions towards his father are dictated more by love than fear. He looks after Hugh with all the consideration of a wife, cooking his food, washing and ironing his clothes, and waiting up for him at night so that he won't fall when he's drunk. When Manus decides to leave Baile Beag, he tries to see that Owen will look after their father, telling him where Hugh's clothes are kept, how he likes his food and how he needs to be looked after at night when he comes home drunk (p. 56).

Manus is single-minded. He gives all his attention to Sarah when he is teaching her to speak but virtually ignores her when he concentrates on Máire or on Hugh (p. 29).

Manus has a good sense of humour and laughs at his own lameness when he tells Máire about Biddy Hanna dictating a letter which included: 'The aul drunken schoolmaster and that lame son of his are still footering about . . .' (p. 16).

There is never one word of criticism about the fact that his father caused his lameness by falling on his cradle when he was a child (p. 37). In fact, it is the opposite: '. . . that's why Manus feels so responsible for him' (p. 37).

Manus is more hostile to the English than either his brother or his father. He understands why Doalty steals the theodolite: 'It was a gesture' (p. 18). He refuses to speak English to Yolland because he suspects that they are witnessing 'a bloody military operation' (p. 32), rather than a peaceful map-making expedition. When he is told that Máire has left the dance with Yolland, he follows them with a stone in his hand, planning to hurt Yolland. When he sees them together, however, he finds that he can do nothing except shout at Yolland in Irish.

Manus eventually manages to get a job and to break away from his father, but only when he has already lost Máire's affection. His last gesture of running away is futile. As Doalty says: 'bloody fool, limping along the coast. They'll overtake him before night' (p. 61).

It is never made clear exactly how much Manus knows about Yolland's disappearance. He follows Máire and Yolland out of the dance and he returns to the dance alone, but whether or not he sees Yolland's abduction is unstated, although the desperate speed with which he wishes to leave Baile Beag suggests that he has reason to avoid being questioned.

Sarah

Sarah is waiflike and described as one who is 'ageless' and could be anything 'from seventeen to thirty-five' (p. 11). She is single and is regarded as dumb by the community in which she lives. Manus encourages her to talk and, under his guidance, she learns to express her identity. She is attracted to Manus, possibly because he is the only one who takes any interest in her, and expresses her affection by bringing him flowers (p. 14). She is aware of Manus's feeling for Máire and tells him about Yolland and Máire leaving the dance (p. 53). Later, she worries that her action may have hurt Manus: 'I'm so sorry, Manus . . .' (p. 57).

Sarah responds well to kindness and finds that she can talk to both Manus and Owen. She is frightened by Lancey and, in spite of encouragement from Owen, cannot tell Lancey her name (p. 62). Sarah's ability to speak parallels and is as short-lived as Yolland's attempt to recreate Irish names in English.

Jimmy Jack

Jimmy Jack Cassie is a bachelor in his sixties; his contemporary, Hugh, addresses him as 'James' (pp. 23 and 65). Jimmy is also called 'Jimmy Jack Cassie' and this is ambiguous, like so much of the naming in the play. It might mean that his surname is 'Cassie' or that he is Cassie's son, Jimmy Jack, or that he is Jimmy son of Jack and grandson of Cassie.

Jimmy Jack is described as being as much at home in the world of Homer as in Baile Beag and is infinitely more interested in the characters in the Classics than in his own comforts. (We are told for example, on p. 11, that he never washes or changes his clothes.) Jimmy is undoubtedly a scholar, but he is relatively uncaring about people. He interrupts Manus when he is encouraging Sarah to talk (pp. 11 and 12) and lacks a sense of humour as shown when he is totally unaware that Doalty is teasing him about being the father of Nellie Ruadh's baby (p. 18). He is right in suggesting that Doalty should set aside some of his land for corn rather than depending on the one crop, potatoes, yet one has some sympathy with Doalty's response: 'Too lazy . . . to wash himself and he's lecturing me on agriculture!'(p. 19)

In Act Three, we learn that Jimmy and Hugh set off to fight for Ireland's independence in the 1798 Rebellion. They left Baile Beag and walked twenty-three miles in one day with Virgil's *Aeneid* in their pockets. They then went into a pub and were so homesick that they forgot about the rebellion and walked home. The grandiose plan of their youth came to nothing, like all their other plans.

By the end of the play, Jimmy has lost the ability to keep his two worlds apart and he informs Hugh that he and Athene are getting married at Christmas (p. 65). The audience is not sure whether his condition is permanent or whether it will pass when he is sober. What is certain is that he is given the task of explaining to Máire the futility of the love between her and Yolland. He sits beside the distracted girl, who talks as if Yolland will come back, and tells her '. . . the word *exogamein* means to marry outside the tribe. And you don't cross those borders casually - both sides get very angry.' (p. 68)

Máire

Máire is described as 'strong-minded', 'strong-bodied' and in her twenties. She must be in her early twenties because Owen, who has been away for six years, comments on the fact that she has grown up: 'It's not − ? . . . it *is* Máire Chatach! God! A young woman!' (p. 26)

Máire is aware of her responsibilities: she would like to marry Manus and stay at home but with ten children younger than her and no father around, Máire must shoulder the burden and go to America (p. 20). Her courage in being willing to go is only matched by her ignorance of what she is letting herself in for. She does not know that Brooklyn is part of a large city and comments 'I hope to God there's no hay to be saved in Brooklyn.' (p. 60)

All of Hugh's pupils are afraid of him but Máire stands up to him, telling him first that she needs to learn English and then defending Daniel O'Connell, whom Hugh dismisses as 'that little Kerry politician' (p. 25). She understands that Manus will not risk offending his father and that he would prefer to lose her than to apply for a post that would guarantee their future. As she tells Manus 'You talk to me about getting married – with neither a roof over your head not a sod of ground under your foot. I suggest you go for the new school; but no . . .' (p. 29).

Máire seems to be the most sympathetic towards the English. She accepts their help at the hay-making (p. 17); she reprimands Doalty for stealing the theodolite (p. 18) and there is an immediate rapport between her and Yolland. They watch each other and overcome all linguistic barriers to express their love. Even this love is, however, based on misunderstanding. Yolland wants to live 'here' with Máire and she wants him to take her away with him (p. 52).

Máire is distraught at the news of Yolland's disappearance. She visits the school to deliver their milk but has forgotten to bring the milk with her. She allows Owen to console her that Yolland will be back and she goes to the hedge-school to wait for him: 'When he comes back, this is where he'll come to. He told me this is where he was happiest.' (p. 68)

Máire is an attractive character, strong and able to make up her own mind. She has a strong sense of family duty and can recognise that Manus does not love her as much as a husband should. She is willing to give up all that she knows for Yolland and we are left not knowing whether or not she will recover, whether or not she will eventually reach America.

Doalty

Daolty is rarely seen on his own and is presented as part of a twosome with Bridget. Usually, he is called 'Doalty' but Hugh calls him 'Doalty Dan Doalty' (p. 24), suggesting that his father is 'Dan' and his grandfather 'Doalty'. He is young, good natured and enjoys teasing people. He is less interested in learning than the others and is shown to be less intelligent, to be, in fact, a 'doer' rather than a 'thinker'; Bridget refers to him as a 'donkey' (p. 18) and he has difficulty learning his tables (p. 24). He is, however, good fun and cleverly mimics Hugh's greeting to the class, 'Vesperal salutations' (pp. 17 and 23), and Hugh's method of structuring his arguments in threes but never getting beyond the second point.

Doalty is given a linguistic mannerism. He says 'Cripes!' when he is excited, worried or flustered and, although he says of Hugh behind his back that '. . . the bugger's hardly fit to walk' (p. 23), he never challenges Hugh's authority or ability to his face.

Doalty harasses the English surveyors by moving their poles and their theodolite. As first, it appears little more than youthful exuberance to see how the engineers react (pp. 17–18); later, we are not so sure. He seems to know more about the Donnelly twins than anyone else in Act One and, in Act Three, he tells Owen that he saw their boat on the night that Yolland was abducted.

His actions may be relatively innocent, but there are hints that he may be more involved in the anti-British action than is ever stated. He never denies knowing where the Donnelly twins are, answering questions by asking another: 'How would I know?' (p. 20). He cut the grass around Yolland's tent and: 'from the tent down to the road' (p. 39). Yolland assumes the action was '. . . so that my feet won't get wet' (p.39) but it may also have been to mark out Yolland's tent so as to facilitate his abduction.

In Act Three, he seems to know that something is going to happen to the British camp and asks Owen to inform Lancey that '. . . his whole camp's on fire' (p. 62) and he tells Owen that he will not allow the English to '. . . put me out without a fight.' (p. 63). He goes off to look for the Donnelly twins, who will know how the young men can defend themselves and the village (p. 64).

Doalty is not an easy character to understand. It is possible that he is simply a light-hearted young man who enjoys poking fun at others. It is also possible, however, that he either intentionally or unintentionally helped in Yolland's abduction.

Bridget

Bridget is a cheerful, intelligent young woman who is closely associated with Doalty. She enjoys a gossip and has learnt a great deal from her brother Seamus. Her information on the national schools is accurate: '. . . you start at the age of six and you have to stick at it until you're twelve at least . . . (p. 22)' and '. . . from the first day you go, you'll not hear one word of Irish' (p. 22) but she sometimes says more than she intends: she knows about the loss of the English horses: '. . . our Seamus says two of the soldiers' horses were found . . .' (p. 20) and about the Donnelly twins, but she stops herself from revealing too much.

Bridget also brings the other pupils news of the potato blight near Cnoc na Mona (p. 21) and has information on Nellie Ruadh's baby, Anna na mBreag's poteen and Owen's way of living in Dublin.

She is not implicated in any of the anti-English activity, but she is with Doalty when they pass Yolland and Máire on the road and when they see the Donnellys' boat. She keeps her eyes and ears open but is unwilling to get involved by giving information about the disappearance of Yolland. 'If you want to know about Yolland, ask the Donnelly twins.' (p. 58)

She is more practical than the men and her first reaction to Lancey's threat to destroy the livestock is: 'We'll have to hide the beasts somewhere – our Seamus'll know where.' (p. 63)

Hugh

Hugh is one of the most important characters in the play and one of the most difficult to assess. He is described as being 'in his early sixties' (p. 23), big, shabby and often intoxicated although not drunk. He is the schoolmaster of the hedge-school, a poet and a linguist. Although no-one doubts his intelligence, local people are beginning to question his competence behind his back. When the play opens, he has sent the children home at eleven o'clock so that he can celebrate the birth of Nellie Ruadh's baby and he is late for the evening class with the adults.

Hugh is dictatorial. He orders Manus around: '. . . a bowl of tea, strong tea, black . . .' (p. 24) and is quite happy to dismiss the class when it suits him. Although he has been in the class for only a few minutes, he tells Owen 'We're finished for the day.' (p. 28) We are not even certain that he is telling the truth when he claims that Mr. Alexander '. . . invited me to take charge of it [the National School] when it opens . . .' (p. 26)

Hugh behaves with great courtesy to Owen and to the English officers: 'You're very welcome, gentlemen.' (p. 30) but he can be sharply critical of his pupils, of Nora Dan whose 'education is complete' because she can now 'write her name' (p. 24) and of Doalty who is described as 'know[ing] nothing' (p. 24). Yet Hugh can combine his sharpness of tongue with a sense of humour, as when he overhears Doalty's description of him as 'the bugger's hardly fit to walk' (p. 23) and comments '*Adsum,* Doalty . . . Perhaps not in *sobrietate perfecta* but adequately *sobrius* to hear your quip.' (p. 23)

Hugh has an interesting relationship with his sons, in both of whom he has inspired a strong sense of love and respect. He depends on Manus yet it is not clear whether he applies for the post in the new National School to blight Manus's marriage prospects or because he assumes that he has a right to it. He has certainly, albeit unintentionally, also maimed Manus by falling on top of his cradle and hurting his leg (p. 37). He welcomes Owen and all those associated with him and yet he asks Owen for money in front of Yolland: 'Can you give me the loan of half-a-crown?' (p. 42) promising to pay it back out of the money he collects to publish a new book, *The Pentaglot Preceptor.* Yolland admires his poetic and linguistic skills, but Owen is more realistic: 'He's bloody pompous.' (p. 43)

Hugh is arrogant and his arrogance can have a nasty side, as when he describes Daniel O'Connell as 'that little Kerry politician' (p. 25) and the

priest as 'a worthy man but barely literate' (p. 41), or it can be innocent, as
when he asks Yolland if the poet Wordsworth had spoken about him: 'Did
he speak of me to you?' (p. 41)

In Act Three, Hugh provides us with insights into his character. His
report of the aborted march with Jimmy Jack in 1798 reveals three points
about Hugh. First, he and Jimmy Jack have more in common than one
might first suspect. Second, he was prepared to leave his wife, '*my* goddess, Caitlin . . . and my infant son in his cradle' (p. 67) for the sake of a
heroic dream. Third, they did not fulfil their ambition but felt homesick
and returned to Baile Beag.

Hugh shows gentleness to both Jimmy Jack and Máire in their distracted
states and promises, at last, to teach Máire the English she wants but 'Not
today. Tomorrow, perhaps.' (p. 67). Like Jimmy Jack, he is too caught up
in a classical world, in his case the Latin world of Ovid's poetry and
Virgil's epic, to bother too much about reality.

The last generalisation that we can make about Hugh is that he has been
given some of the finest lines and some of the most interesting ideas in the
play. It is he who tells Captain Lancey that English is ideally suited to
commerce (p. 25), and informs Yolland about the riches of the Irish
language being, perhaps, a response to 'mud cabins and a diet of potatoes',
and finally, he warns Máire that he will teach her English but that the
words and the grammar may not empower her 'to interpret between
privacies' (p. 67).

Owen

Owen is Hugh's second son, a handsome man in his twenties (p. 26). He
managed to escape from Baile Beag six years earlier but did not find the
streets of Dublin paved with gold, in spite of the rumours of his great
wealth.

He is courteous to everyone, women and men, locals and visitors alike
and he shows both affection for and knowledge of his father. For example,
he overlooks his father's weakness for alcohol and tries to look after his
needs when Manus leaves and yet he knows that Hugh can be pompous
(p. 43) and that he can often be carried away by the sound of his own
voice: 'Will you stop that nonsense, Father' (p. 42) and: 'Enduring around
truths immemorially posited – hah!' (p. 43)

Owen is kind to Sarah and, like Manus, can encourage her to talk
(p. 28); he is fond of Yolland and tries to warn him not to have romantic
ideas about Ireland (p. 43); he tries to safeguard Manus by telling him not
to leave in suspicious circumstances (p. 55) and then offers him money
(p. 56); and he is gentle to Máire, assuring her that Yolland will 'turn up'
(p. 60). Early in the play, he takes the easy way out by not translating
Lancey's description of the reason for the expedition (p. 31) but, in the

final act, he decides to join Doalty and the young men in their attempt to counteract Lancey's threats: 'I've got to go. I've got to see Doalty Dan Doalty.' (p. 66).

Owen is a middleman and plays a part in bridging the two cultures. Like many middlemen, however, his contribution to the chaos that engulfs Baile Beag is not easy to evaluate. For him, the English substitution of 'Roland' for 'Owen' is insignificant, although readers of the play may see it as an unwillingness to insist on accuracy, or even justice.

Captain Lancey

Captain Lancey is almost a stereotype of the stiff, unyielding British officer. He genuinely believes that any nation is blessed to be part of the British Empire: '. . . Ireland is privileged' (p. 31). He is a conscientious officer. At the end of his day, he personally 'met every group of sappers as they reported in.' He personally checked the field kitchens and examined every single report (p. 39).

He is, as Yolland tells us, 'the perfect colonial servant' (p. 39) and every job must be performed 'with excellence' (p. 40). He and his men finish the surveying quickly and are only held up by Yolland's love of Baile Beag.

Lancey has no curiosity about local places and customs. He does the job he is given with energy and enthusiasm. He is absolutely honest about his intentions although Owen does not translate them accurately (p. 31). He warns the local people about harassment and threatens an escalating plan of destruction if Yolland is not found. He promises that, within twenty-four hours, all the livestock in Ballybeg will be destroyed and, within forty-eight hours he and his soldiers will begin a campaign of eviction that will affect every home in the area (p. 61).

Captain Lancey is firm and unyielding. He gives a warning of his intentions, but he is prepared to 'ravish the whole parish' if Yolland is not returned. No-one doubts that Lancey will keep his promise or that many will suffer for the actions of a few.

People in the locality understand Captain Lancey. As Manus says 'I understand the Lanceys perfectly but people like you [that is, Yolland] puzzle me.' (p. 37)

Lieutenant Yolland

There is a small factual problem about Yolland which may simply be a slip. On p. 30, Yolland is described as being in his late twenties or early thirties but Yolland tells Owen that his father was born on July 14, 1789 (p. 40). This means that Yolland's father is 44, a fact that would make it impossible for him to have a 30-year-old son. If we are to believe the date provided by Yolland, then he is unlikely to be more than 20 or 21 and, indeed, his actions are more in keeping with this age.

Yolland, like Lancey, is introduced by his surname, but we soon learn that his first name is George (p. 32) and that he and Owen travelled together from Dublin (p. 28). Yolland is courteous to everyone he meets. He is not a gifted speaker but he expresses his affection for Ireland and the language: 'I feel ... foolish to – to – be working here and not to speak your language ... I think your countryside is ... beautiful. I've fallen in love with it already ...' (p. 32). Within a few days he has learnt more about Irish culture and linguistic traditions – and poteen – than Lancey would ever want to learn.

Yolland describes himself as something of a failure and, indeed, his most frequently used word is 'sorry'. His father is, like Lancey, energetic, able, fair but unyielding, and Yolland was a disappointment to him. It was Yolland's father who eventually got Yolland a job in India but Yolland missed the boat and joined the army as a means of escaping his father's wrath (p. 39). He is immediately attracted to Baile Beag: 'I know that I'm going to be happy ... here' (p. 32) and is also attracted to Máire. He speaks to her when they first meet (p. 32), watches her and her house from his tent: 'I hear music coming from that house nearly every night' (p. 38) and he is ecstatic when Máire invites him to a dance and shouts out the Irish names he has learnt (p. 48).

Yolland, unlike Lancey, is impressed that Hugh and Jimmy Jack can converse in Greek and Latin, and when Owen describes his father as 'pompous', Yolland prefers to call him 'astute' (p. 43).

Some critics have argued that Yolland is an unrealistic character and that it is unlikely that a young British officer would, in 1833, fall in love with a peasant girl and want to settle down in Baile Beag. Yet, if he is about twenty, then his romantic attraction is much more comprehensible.

Yolland is gentle, courteous, romantic and yet there is also a core of realism in him. He knows that even if he did learn Irish, and even if he did settle down in Baile Beag, he would probably always feel, and would always be regarded as, an outsider (p. 40).

Family Relationships

Family relationships are always significant in Irish literature, where the mother figure often dominates. In *Translations*, we see the father/son relationships of Hugh and his two sons and we hear about Yolland's attitude to his real father and to Lancey who reminds him of his father; we learn about Máire's sense of responsibility for the ten children younger than her; we are made aware of Bridget's closeness to 'our Seamus'; the Donnelly twins are so close that they function as one, undifferentiated entity. The relationships in *Translations* are strong but, in so far as we can see, they are sterile and all of the characters are single or unattached. The one mention of new life is Nellie Ruadh's baby, but even here there are problems: the father's identity is uncertain and the child dies within a few days.

Significance of the Famine

The potato was introduced into Ireland by Sir Walter Raleigh (?1552–1618). It rapidly became the main food of the Irish people, whose poverty was commented on by many writers, including Jonathan Swift (1667–1745) in such essays as 'A Modest Proposal'. By the nineteenth century, the Catholic population of Ireland depended almost entirely on a diet of potatoes, milk and fish. Many grew corn on the better land but the Corn Laws of 1806 meant that the corn had to be sent to England.

Cases of potato blight are recorded in Ireland from the eighteenth century but the blight tended to affect only certain areas. In 1845, the weather conditions were such that the blight affected potatoes throughout Ireland. The Great Famine that resulted caused the death of approximately one in every three people and the emigration of thousands more.

It would be hard to overestimate the significance of the 'Great Hunger' in Irish tradition. The fears expressed by Bridget in Act 1 of *Translations* are, perhaps, anachronistic in that the full horrors of a famine were not felt in Ireland until the mid 1840s.

Significance of the setting

We have dealt briefly with this in the Introduction, but now that we have studied the background, structure and characters in greater detail, it is possible to pay a little more attention to the setting and, in particular, to the likelihood that people in a hedge-school in 1833 would be fluent in Greek and Latin.

Hedge-schools were often established in rural areas of Ireland to teach Catholics, mainly, to read, write and do arithmetic, and indeed, these subjects are taught in Baile Beag, as Bridget makes clear when she gives Hugh her money: 'There's the one-and-eight I owe you for . . . arithmetic and there's my one-and-six for . . . writing' (p. 24).

Many traditional stories abound regarding the high quality of education available in such schools and many of these stories are, we may assume, exaggerated. It is likely that some Irish scholars knew Greek and Latin and carried copies of the Classics in their pockets. It is also likely that many more were lucky to be literate in their own language.

In setting the play in a remote area of Donegal where the peasant pupils conversed easily in Irish, Greek and Latin, Friel is not trying to recreate naturalistic village life in Ireland in the 1830s. Rather, he is stressing that the English were not bringing civilisation with them but were in contact with people who had their own language, their own culture, their own traditions and their own educational ideals and aspirations.

We might argue that it is unlikely that the English officers knew no Latin; all educated Englishmen studied Latin in the nineteenth century. Having studied it at school, however, does not mean that one could automatically use it as a link language.

General comments

Translations is a play dealing with language, with contacts between people who do not speak the same language or share the same aspirations. It is a play about alienation, about relationships, about a small community and its limitations, about love and about the long struggle between the English and the Irish. It is, in many ways, a pessimistic play, suggesting that love cannot triumph over prejudice, that education is only of value if it is practical, that the English and the Irish are almost fated to repeat cycles of misunderstanding: 'When my grandfather was a boy, they did the same thing.' (p. 63) and that Ireland's language and culture are doomed because of invasion and also because: '. . . it can happen that a civilisation can be imprisoned in a linguistic contour that no longer matches the landscape of . . . fact.' (p. 43)

Part 4

Hints for study

How to approach the play

Drama and poetry are most fully appreciated when spoken aloud, and drama is best appreciated as a stage performance where words, actions, setting and characters combine to create an impact which is both aural and visual. A play, like a novel, can tell a story, often involving many characters and the passage of time, but its uniqueness lies in its ability to create an alternative universe in which a member of the audience can observe the enactment of events that parallel events in their own lives or histories.

How to analyse plays

Ideally, we should see a play, but in this section we shall examine *Translations* as a written text.

Although there are no simple rules that will work on every occasion, there are three general comments that should help. The first is to realise that understanding is based on three stages:

* reading and responding to the play
* checking your response by close reference to the text
* evaluating the play.

Often, when we read a play, we are not absolutely certain of the writer's intentions. We can, of course, clearly perceive the main events in the story; we can recognise strongly-held opinions on politics, perhaps, or on the relationship between the English and the Irish. We can also, however, react to aspects of a play on an emotional level, before we respond to them intellectually. We gradually learn about translation, for example, because it is going on at every level and in every section of the play. Jimmy Jack translates from Greek into Irish; Hugh asks his pupils to translate to and from Latin and Greek; Owen translates Irish placenames for Yolland and he also translates Lancey's announcements for those in the hedge-school. We gradually learn how impossible it is to express a culture by means of another language. We also become aware of the menace that hangs over Baile Beag and that is communicated as much by images of the potato famine as by the threats of Captain Lancey.

When we have noted our responses to events and characters, we should check to see if we can support or refine them. If we have sensed desperation in the play, for example, is it because of the story, or because of our identification with a particular character, or because of the words and imagery used? Or is it, indeed, a fusion of all three? Are the characters fulfilled? Do they seek an escape in poetry? in alcohol? in love? in exile? Do the characters understand each other? Is the language they use naturalistic? Do words get in the way? Is the deepest understanding expressed without language? Do we identify more readily with Máire and Yolland because we can respond more easily to human love than to the discipline of Lancey or the poetry of Hugh? Do we, in fact, feel that the play's outcome is inevitable because we have, at some level, noticed the repeated references to impending disaster? the repeated references to the shadowy Donnelly twins?

By this stage, we have begun to evaluate the play, assessing how effectively the dramatist controls story, characters, dialogue and images and, through them, our response. The evaluation should not be either mechanical or superficial. It should always be based on our own reactions, reactions which have been informed by a close reading of the text. We should avoid sweeping generalisations. The play certainly has parallels with the recent history of Northern Ireland, but is not simply a barely disguised commentary on the British in Northern Ireland. It will be useful for us to remind ourselves that a history play is not history and so must not be judged by the same criteria as history.

We should also remember that, in our comments, we are offering an interpretation of a play, and that an interpretation is always partial, never complete. That explains why two people can respond strongly, yet differently, to the same work. It is perfectly feasible that one reader will regard Hugh as a drunken tyrannical father who has ruined his own life and is doing a good job of ruining his son's, while another may see his life as a waste of talent and opportunity, a man who might have been great had he not been trapped in Baile Beag. As long as we can support our point of view by reference to the text, our evaluation will be valid.

How to write about *Translations*

Each of us, with practice, evolves our own style. In writing about literature, however, it may be useful to employ a number of strategies. These are meant as a support for your ideas, not as a substitute for them.

Having read the play, thought about it and discussed your views, you may feel that it is helpful to write about some or all of its themes. With a play, it is usually helpful to consider the story, the characters, the setting, the structure, the dialogue and the imagery.

First, let us take the level of story. Briefly, *Translations* deals with a society at a point in its history when change is inevitable. The change will be triggered by two events:

- the intervention of an army-led ordnance team that plans to map and name every significant hill and valley in the region and
- the opening of an English-medium National School.

These changes are introduced against a backdrop of misunderstanding and mistrust, love and loyalty, family relationships and a gradual awareness that pain and violence are experienced in almost every generation in both the region and the country.

At one level, the play describes one aspect of the contact between the English and the Irish and their inability or unwillingness to understand each other. At another, it describes the meeting of a young Irishwoman and an English officer, their love, their attempts to communicate and their brutal separation. Their ability to communicate intuitively is in stark contrast to the more general misunderstanding between the English and the Irish.

Secondly, we should examine the characters. We can do this mainly by examining their actions, by what they say about themselves and what others say about them. In a play, there is no narrator who can provide information which we know to be reliable. A play is closer to real life in that we meet people, we hear what they say, we see what they do and we make up our minds about them. Sometimes we are wrong in our first judgements, which may need to be reassessed in the light of subsequent behaviour. It is certainly true that many characters in *Translations* are utterly realistic in that they are hard to evaluate. Should we admire Hugh? He is certainly given the best lines in the play and his wit and intelligence are unquestionable. But can we overlook his drinking, his treatment of his son, his arrogance? Perhaps it is a positive comment on the playwright's ability to create lifelike characters if we cannot categorise them easily.

Thirdly, we should think of the settings of the play and, in particular, of the contrast between the educated peasants and the less well educated invaders. We should think also of the poverty of the region, the need for people like Máire to leave home in order to earn money, and the menace of the potato blight that is always close, always threatening to devastate the crops. It does not matter, perhaps, that the hedge-school setting is unlikely to be as adept at producing classical scholars as *Translations* suggests. What does matter is that the characters make the audience believe that it is real.

Fourthly, it may be of value to consider the structure of the play. Is the setting sufficiently unusual to make us 'willingly suspend our disbelief'? Is the convention that most of the characters are speaking Irish convincing? If so, how does Friel achieve this? If not, why and how does it fail? Is the dialogue realistic? Is the play aimed at a young audience, an older audience? at an Irish audience? at an English audience? at both? Is it likely that different audiences would draw different conclusions from the play? Would they all be valid? The only way to answer any of these questions is to know the play intimately and to think about how it is constructed. In a short play like this every word, every structure, everything reported and everything omitted is of significance. Don't assume anything and don't be misled by critics, even influential ones. Some critics have argued that *Translations* is a thinly disguised criticism of the stationing of British troops in Northern Ireland from 1969. Others feel that it is of much wider significance than this and that, in leaving the twentieth century, Friel was able to devote himself to the pursuit of universal truths.

Fifthly, we should examine the dialogue closely. A dramatist relies heavily on the naturalness of the speech to mould the audience's response to characters and events. Friel takes trouble to create the impression of live speech. Hugh is characterised by his love of elegant language, 'I encountered Captain Lancey ... and to his credit he seemed suitably verecund' (pp. 24–25); and the Irish characters use words and structures that emphasise their similarity to each other and their difference from the English:

BRIDGET: God but you're a dose. (p. 20)
MÁIRE: For God's sake, sure you know he'd never – (p. 21)
LANCEY: His Majesty's government has ordered the first ever comprehensive survey of this entire country ... (p. 31)

Only once do the differences between the speech of Irish and English characters seem to blur and that is when Yolland and Máire are communicating in spite of language difficulties:

MÁIRE: The grass must be wet. My feet are soaking.
YOLLAND: Your feet must be wet. The grass is soaking. (p. 49)

but, even here, their ways of viewing events are different. Máire realises that the grass must be wet because her feet are soaking; Yolland deduces that her feet must be wet because the grass is soaking.

Finally, we should be aware that a writer's imagery can influence us, even before we fully understand how or why. When we think that a play is gentle or violent, angry or composed, contemporary or old fashioned, sexist or politically correct, we are sometimes responding to the playwright's use of imagery. *Translations* has recurrent interrelated images of light, dark, love, money, rich harvest and potential blight, hope and despair, ignorance and learning, religion, life, death, hardship and escapism. They are associated with people and their moods, and with places and their associations, and with the knowledge that *Sic transit gloria mundi* (This is how the glory of the world passes). 'Tobair Vree' (p. 43), for example, is a poorly remembered form of 'Brian's Well', but by the time Owen and Yolland are translating, the well has disappeared, Brian's pain and death have been forgotten and even his name has been 'corrupted' (p. 43).

Answering questions on *Translations*

There is no set of mechanical rules which we can follow in preparing to answer questions on any writer. The most useful piece of advice is to know the text. Read it; think about it; talk about it; try to understand it. When it comes to answering essay questions or examination topics, it is advisable to keep the following points in mind:

* Read the question carefully, ensuring that you know exactly what is required of you.
* Plan your answer in points before writing your essay. A good essay will have an introductory paragraph devoted to a consideration of the topic, separate paragraphs on each of the points you make, and a concluding paragraph evaluating the topic from your point of view.
* Use quotations, even one- or two-word quotations, in support of your opinion. There is, of course, no need to quote the page reference in an examination, although it may be a useful scholarly exercise in project work. Page references are supplied in these notes to help you find the quotations easily.
* Write simply, clearly and honestly. There is no particular merit in long sentences and polysyllabic words. Examiners are interested in your views on *Translations*, rather than in those of teachers or critics.
* Remember that although the characters in the play are meant to be lifelike, they are not real people. Do not worry unduly about what happened before or after the events related in the play itself.
* Always re-read your essays. If you cannot understand what you have written, no one else will.
* Present your work neatly.

Sample questions and suggested answers

Before presenting a number of essay topics and suggested responses, there are two points to stress:

* It is neither useful nor desirable to offer students a set of 'model' answers, since over-reliance on such answers can limit original thinking and discourage you from using your own knowledge and ideas creatively.
* These notes are intended to train minds, not memories. We encourage you, therefore, to think about everything we have said and to evaluate it.

Nevertheless, it may be helpful to indicate how a student might deal with a topic, and so one full sample essay is provided, together with two essay plans. If you disagree with some of the points made, that is good, but notice that the subject is dealt with logically and systematically.

1. 'It is impossible to appreciate *Translations* fully without having detailed knowledge of the social and linguistic history of Ireland.' Discuss

PLAN
Introductory paragraph
What is meant by 'appreciate fully'?
   Can we only partly appreciate the story if we do not know anything about the social or linguistic history of Ireland?
   Can we appreciate *Translations* more, although differently, if we know a lot about Ireland's history?
   Is it perhaps a criticism of *Translations* to suggest that it is in some way incomplete, or that it must be studied as historical or linguistic data?

Body of essay
It is certainly easier to understand *Translations* on first reading if we are aware of the long history of contact and misunderstanding between the English and the Irish, and if we know something about Irish and Irish English.
   It is also possible to respond to the power of the language, the ideas and the characters, even if we have never heard of Daniel O'Connell and Catholic Emancipation, or of the influences of Irish Gaelic on the English language in Ireland.
   If *Translations* depended on a knowledge of history and language, then without this knowledge it would be incomplete, a mere fragment of what we need to know to respond to it. This is not true.

Conclusion
Translations can be appreciated without our knowing anything about the social and linguistic history of Ireland. There are even positive reasons why we should examine it in and for itself without reference to extraneous information. Friel's achievement in *Translations* is that he makes his audience think about human rather than merely 'Irish' experiences. It is undoubtedly true that any historical and linguistic information we carry to the play *may* deepen our response to it, but such 'baggage' may also cause us to recreate the play to fit a particular point of view, rather than to respond to it as it is.

ESSAY
When critics talk about our trying to 'appreciate' any play 'fully', they presumably mean that the more background information we possess about playwrights, their history, their interests and preoccupations, the closer we can come to sharing in the 'full' meaning of their dramatic creations. Such a view can, however, be challenged on at least two counts. First, we know very little about Shakespeare, for example, but *Hamlet* remains one of the

most intriguing plays in English and, whilst interpretations may change
over time, the challenge of the play has not diminished. Secondly, every
dramatic performance is an interpretation, created by the combined talents
of playwright, performers and audience. To suggest that any one produc-
tion or reception would result in 'full appreciation' is perhaps to think of a
play as a container with a determined set of contents rather than as an
organic piece of art that changes as people change. Readers or members of
an audience may react differently if they understand the social, linguistic
and historical background to the play, but different responses cannot be
equated with fuller appreciation.

To begin with, let us take an extreme case. If we approached *Translations* knowing nothing of hedge-schools or life in Ireland during the
1830s, if we had never heard of Daniel O'Connell or British occupation, if
we were totally ignorant of National Schools or the Great Famine, and if
we had never thought about Irish Gaelic or its replacement by English,
would we be able to respond to the play? The answer is likely to be
positive. Any modern audience can respond to ideas of education, armies
of occupation, family relationships, love and terrorism, whether the setting
is in Ireland or Nigeria. If a play is to have more than local significance,
its action and themes must transcend the regional. We must be able to
respond to it even if we are unaware of some of the cultural and linguistic
references. We do not, for example, need to know anything about the
syntactic intricacies of Irish Gaelic to understand Hugh's claim that it is:
'... a rich language ... full of the mythologies of fantasy and hope and
self-deception – a syntax opulent with tomorrows. It is our response to
mud cabins and a diet of potatoes ...' (p. 42).

On the other hand, *Translations* is not written entirely in standard
English. The playwright deliberately makes use of a form of English
which is not stereotypically 'stage Irish' but which uses words and phrases
that most people associate with Ireland. We notice the frequent use of
'sure' and reflexive pronoun, 'Sure you know I have only Irish like
yourself' (p. 16); we respond to Irish pronunciations like 'aul eejit' (p. 17)
and the frequent references to God, 'Be God, that's my territory alright'
(p. 19), but these are all readily comprehensible to speakers of any variety
of English, and most people would understand the implication of Hugh
being 'on the batter since this morning' (p. 17) even if they were unaware
that 'batter' probably comes from the Irish word 'bother', meaning 'road'.

As well as using a regionally marked form of English, Brian Friel
intersperses historical information. He mentions Daniel O'Connell, the
'Liberator' (p. 25) and tells us through Hugh that he is a 'Kerry politician'
(p. 25). This piece of information undervalues O'Connell's achievements
but it prevents any reader or member of an audience losing the thread of
the story. Friel uses historical figures such as O'Connell, and historical
facts like the Storming of the Bastille in Paris in July 1789 (p. 40) to

locate his drama in a particular place and time. It is useful if we have a knowledge of such characters and events, but the dramatist provides us with the information we need to respond to his characters and their dialogue.

Each of us approaches a piece of literature with different amounts of knowledge, differing degrees of sensitivity. We may well appreciate a modern sonnet more if we have read earlier sonnets, but ignorance of earlier examples should not cause a failure of response. We will respond as fully as we can, at that particular time, to the piece of literature being studied. Our response will almost certainly change as we change because great writings appeal to us differently at different stages of our lives.

Any reader or any member of an audience can respond to *Translations* without a sophisticated knowledge of its background and, indeed, if *Translations* depended for its appeal on a given amount of knowledge of history and language, then it would be incomplete, a fragment of what we need to know to respond to it. Friel could, however, assume that contemporary audiences would know a considerable amount about Northern Ireland, and he would certainly hope that his play would encourage people to think more deeply about issues that they had previously ignored.

---

2. Write a detailed analysis of Hugh's character, indicating why you think he is central to *Translations*

PLAN

For this type of essay, you should remember that an evaluation of any character depends on an analysis of:
   what the character says
   what the character does
   what other people say about the character.

Introductory paragraph
Comment briefly on Hugh's status in the community, his appearance in all three Acts, his undoubted intelligence and the fact that the last words in the play are given to him.

Body of essay
What do Hugh's words reveal about himself? Is he considerate of and courteous to Manus? his pupils? the English visitors? Does he consider the needs of other people? Is he thoughtful? Is he brave? Has he got a sense of humour? Is he arrogant? Is he self-deceived? Is he likeable?

What do Hugh's actions reveal about him? Does he try to teach the pupils subjects that will be of use to them? Does he look after his home and family? Does he try to curb his drinking? Is he a good communicator? Does he believe what he says?

'What do other people say or think about him? Manus loves him and tries to see that he will be looked after even when he has left Baile Beag. Owen is genuinely fond of him but suggests that he is 'pompous'. Most of the pupils are frightened of him but do not show him much respect. Yolland admires his linguistic skills and his astuteness.

Conclusion
Hugh is a complex character. We can admire his intelligence and his eloquence but has he wasted his talents and his life?

3. Brian Friel's *Translations* deals with 'the linguistic crisis which saw the disappearance of Gaelic and its replacement by English' (Seamus Deane). How far do you agree with this assessment of the play?

PLAN
Remember that there are three parts to this question. You must say what you think Deane meant by his claim; in particular, you must say whether the play suggests that the disappearance of Gaelic was due to a 'linguistic' crisis, a social crisis or was, perhaps, inevitable; and you should evaluate whether or not such a description does justice to the subtlety of the play.

Introductory paragraph
Concentrate first on the linguistic issues in the play: the pupils are skilled in Latin, Greek and Irish Gaelic but remain extremely poor and need English if they are to compete even with the Buncrana people; Irish Gaelic is perfectly capable of dealing with life in Baile Beag but is Baile Beag not a backwater? Is the trouble caused by linguistic differences? Secondly, suggest that the play may be more deeply philosophical and universal than Deane's comment suggests.

Body of Essay
Translations deals, primarily, with the thoughts and actions of Gaelic-speaking people in their contact with a party of English soldiers who are attempting to produce a precise map of their region. As the title might suggest, a great deal of the conversation involves translation: translation of Greek and Latin texts into Gaelic in the hedge-school; translation of Irish placenames into English for the purposes of map-making.

There is also much discussion of the nature of the languages coming into contact and of the difficulties involved even in translating placenames.

The play certainly suggests that English will replace Gaelic: the locals recognise the need for it; the National Schools will not permit any language other than English; and the power is in the hands of the English-speaking soldiers. Yet the disappearance of Gaelic is not just the result of conquest. Hugh implies that Irish Gaelic is *doomed* when he describes it as '... a rich language ... full of the mythologies of fantasy and hope and self-deception – a syntax opulent with tomorrows' (p. 42). English may, in Hugh's estimation, be best suited 'for the purposes of commerce' (p. 25) but commerce is wealth-creating, whereas a language that deals admirably with 'tomorrows' may be unsatisfactory in coping with 'today'. And, throughout the play, there is the sense of impending danger that will come not directly from conquest or language use but from a blight on the potato crop.

However, the play is concerned with much more than a 'linguistic crisis'. It deals with problems of communication between one generation and the next and between the English and the Irish. It deals with love, instability, deceit, treachery and tragedy.

Conclusion

To reduce any play of distinction to one theme or to suggest that it can be summed up in one phrase is to undervalue it. A great play will reflect the issues and preoccupations of both its writer and its age, but it will also transcend them. In *Translations*, Brian Friel tackles the topic of the loss of Irish Gaelic and the associated loss of culture, but he uses this topic to explore the relationship between the English and the Irish, in the present as well as in 1833; the relationship between people of different ages and different genders; the self-destructive urges that can result in both barbarism and impressive courage; and the suffering that misunderstandings can cause.

Revision questions

The following questions should help you in your work on *Translations*. For ease of use, we shall divide them into two categories: General and Particular.

General

1. *Translations* poses the question 'Why do such terrible things as murder and revenge occur in life?' Does Brian Friel provide his audience with any answers to this question?
2. Describe and discuss Brian Friel's major skills as a playwright. (Remember to consider the plot, the characters and the dialogue.)
3. 'Brian Friel writes about love and loyalty, family relationships, interaction between the individual and the community.' Is this an accurate assessment of *Translations*?
4. Brian Friel writes about suffering and alienation. Does this mean we can classify him as a 'depressing' writer? Support your answer by close reference to *Translations*.

5. '*Translations* is a deeply pessimistic play. It questions the value of an education that is not goal-oriented; it suggests that the English and the Irish cannot and will not understand each other; and it implies that love is less powerful than hate.' Do you agree?
6. Examine the claim that *Translations* has no hero and no heroine because none of the characters has heroic stature.
7. 'Part of the power of *Translations* comes from the use of echoes. Sarah's problem with speech resembles the community's inability to use a language that will allow them to communicate with the outside world; Jimmy Jack's absorption into the life of classical Greek is paralleled by Hugh's love of classical Rome; Lancey's behaviour repeats the behaviour of other English officers two generations before.' Do you agree with this statement? Support your answer by close analysis of the play.
8. Illustrate and discuss Friel's views on love and loyalty.
9. 'Although Máire and Yolland seem very different, their actions stem from a similar need to escape from the life they have known.' Discuss.
10. Examine Friel's preoccupation with one or more of the following motifs: the father/son relationship; the interaction between the individual and the community; intellectual wealth and social poverty; the fear of the unknown; the influence of one's language and/or surroundings on one's behaviour.

Particular

1. Explain the role of Owen in *Translations*.
2. Compare the characters of Hugh and Jimmy Jack. Did their study of the classics condition them to accept their poverty without question or did their characters encourage them to find escapism in the classics?
3. Give an account of Manus's behaviour to Sarah, Máire and Yolland.
4. Describe and discuss the relationships between Yolland and Owen and Yolland and Máire.
5. 'One of the themes of *Translations* is the loss of one's grip on reality.' Discuss this view with relation to one of the following: Hugh, Jimmy Jack, Máire, Yolland.
6. 'Máire and Yolland are as different as the landscapes of their childhoods.' What validity is there in such a claim?
7. 'Manus is his father's son. They both waste their talents and opportunities.' Discuss.
8. Discuss the value of using hibernicised English for some of the characters in *Translations*.
9. What part is played in the development of the plot by the following characters: Bridget, Doalty, the Donnelly twins, Lancey and Sarah?

10. 'In spite of the potential intimacy offered by a play, we never learn what any of the characters really think.' Discuss this claim in connection with Máire or Manus or Yolland.

Topics for classroom discussion

When we first read *Translations*, it may seem simple and straightforward. A closer reading, however, reveals that the simplicity is not 'natural' or 'spontaneous' but the result of crafted artistry. No detail is provided without a reason. Within the first few minutes of the play, for example, we are told that Máire is interested in English and that she knows a few words 'In Norfolk we besport ourselves around the maypoll' (p. 15). This simple saying links Máire with Yolland, who comes from Norfolk (p. 60). Their fates are intimately linked even before they meet.

Similar points may be made about every character and, indeed, every action. Initially, we may see Jimmy Jack as totally individualistic in his love of the classics. Later, we see that he and Hugh have much in common, that both find a fulfilment in their books that they have not found in life. Nor do the similarities end there. Jimmy Jack and Hugh went off to war with the Aeneid in their pocket; Manus leaves Baile Beag and any chance of a life with Máire, carrying copies of Virgil, Caesar and Aeschylus (p. 56).

Brian Friel's greatest achievement in this play is that he leaves room for doubt and discussion. Your appreciation of the play will be deepened if you discuss some, or all, of the following topics:

1. Losing one's grip on reality is one of the themes of the play. How would you describe this? Is it akin to madness? Does Jimmy Jack finally lose the ability to distinguish real life from fiction? Will Máire ever recover from the distraction she feels? Does Friel perhaps suggest that the only way of dealing with an unpalatable life is to seek a virtual existence in literature or in dreams? Is there a parallel between this and Hugh's comment: 'A rich language [that is, Irish Gaelic]. A rich literature. You'll find, sir, that certain cultures expend on their [languages] energies and ostentations lacking in their material lives.'

2. What is Friel's attitude to the Irish language and its literature? Does he feel that the English language was as destructive as the potato blight? Are you sure? Is there not evidence in the play that Friel felt that an unchanging language or society led to stagnation? What is Friel's purpose in making Hugh claim that the Irish 'feel closer to the warm Mediterranean' in terms of language and literature? Are we justified in assuming that Hugh expressed Friel's opinion?

3. Friel has acknowledged an influence from George Steiner. Below, we provide a number of quotations from Steiner's *After Babel*. How

influential do you think they were in shaping the play? If these were Steiner's views, can we claim that the actions and views expressed in *Translations* relate more to human society in general than to Ireland in particular?

- 'In certain civilizations there come epochs in which syntax stiffens . . . Instead of acting as a living membrane, grammar and vocabulary become a barrier to new feeling' (p. 21).
- 'When we read or hear any . . . statement from the past, be it Leviticus or last year's best seller, we translate' (p. 28).
- 'To remember everything is a condition of madness.' (p. 29).
- 'To remember is to risk despair; the past tense of the verb to be must infer the reality of death' (p. 30).
- '. . . children know that silence can destroy another human being' (p. 35).
- 'Each [dying language] takes with it a storehouse of consciousness' (p. 54).
- 'There appears to be no correlation between linguistic wealth and other resources of a community,' (p. 55).
- '. . . real translation is impossible. What passes for translation is a convention of rough-cast similitude . . .' (p. 74).
- 'Whorf's theses are well known. Linguistic patterns determine what the individual perceives in his world and how he thinks about it' (p. 88).
- 'The point is always the same: ash is no translation of fire' (p. 241).

4. Many plays deal with love and politics. How does Friel manage to give these subjects a new lease of life in *Translations?* What is the significance of the fact that Sarah loves Manus who loves Máire who loves Yolland? Why does Friel go to so much trouble to stress Lancey's good points: his industry? his fairness? his sense of discipline?
5. Read John Montague's poem 'A Grafted Tongue' and consider its applicability to *Translations.* Below, we quote a few lines:

> . . . Dumb,
> bloodied, the severed
> head now chokes to
> speak another tongue . . .
> As in
> a long suppressed dream . . .
> An Irish
> child weeps at school
> repeating its English . . .
> Decades later

that child's grandchild's
speech stumbles over lost
syllables of an old order.

6. Examine the proportions of the play. What is the significance of the different lengths of acts and the fact that each act is shorter than the previous one?
7. Is *Translations* a political play? If you believe that it is, do you think that such a classification is a criticism? If you think it is not a political play, or not just a political play, how is it saved from being classified as such? (Do the brevity of the play and the uncertainties that are not resolved have any bearing on this topic?)
8. Many people have claimed that *Translations* is a play that appeals mainly to an audience with Irish sympathies. Do you think that this is true? partly? completely? If you do, do you think this is a weakness? If you think that *Translations* appeals also and/or equally to audiences of any political or ethnic background, explain why this is so.
9. Most playwrights have avoided using non-standard English for any of the main characters in their novels. Why? Is correctness of speech, in some way, associated with intelligence or moral rectitude? Friel uses not only dialectal English for some speakers but also Greek and Latin, for which the audience would have no immediate translation. Why? What dramatic advantages did he gain by using such variation? Discuss the view that, in *Translations*, the dialect is the voice of intimacy.
10. Has *Translations* caused you to think in a new way about such subjects as language, translation, education, rejection, parent–child relationships, the relationship between the Irish and the English? If so, do you think of this as a mark of a great play? Should a play make us think about such subjects? Would they be better treated in a social tract? Is 'better' the same as 'more memorable'? Perhaps we should leave the last words to Steiner: 'To know more of language and translation, we must pass from the "deep structures" of transformational grammar to the deeper structures of the poet' (p. 108).

Part 5
Suggestions for further reading

The text

FRIEL, BRIAN: *Translations*, Faber and Faber, London, 1981.

Brian Friel's plays

In particular, you should try to read *Dancing at Lughnasa* (1990). This play is also set in Ballybeg, but in 1936, just over a hundred years after the action depicted in *Translations* (1833). In *Translations*, we see the beginnings of the influence of the English language and educational system on the inhabitants of a small town in Donegal. By 1936, the Engish language has completely ousted Irish Gaelic and the influence of the outside world via the media is beginning to affect and displace the local culture. The later play also takes place in the month of August or Mí na Lughnasa, when a harvest is about to begin. The meaning of 'harvest' in both plays is both literal and symbolic.

Bibliographical and critical studies

CONNOLLY, S.: 'Dreaming History: Brian Friel's *Translations*', *Theatre Ireland 13*, Autumn 1987, pp. 42–4.

DANTANUS, U.: *Brian Friel: The Growth of an Irish Dramatist*, Humanities Press, New Jersey, 1986.

DEANE, S.: 'The Double Stage', *Celtic Revivals: Essays in Modern Irish Literature*, Faber and Faber, London, 1985, pp. 166–73.

FOSTER, R. F.: *Modern Ireland 1600–1972*, Allen Lane, Penguin, London, 1988.

HINDLEY, R.: *The Death of the Irish Language*, Routledge, London, 1990.

KEARNEY, R.: 'Language Play: Brian Friel and Ireland's Verbal Theatre', *Studies 72*, Spring 1983, pp. 20–56.

KEY, R.: *Ireland: A history*, Sphere Books, Abacus edition, London, 1980.

MAXWELL, D. E. S.: *A Critical History of Modern Irish Drama, 1891–1980*, Cambridge University Press, Cambridge, 1984.

O'BRIEN, G.: *Brian Friel*, Gill and Macmillan, Dublin, 1989.

O'BRIEN, M. and CRUISE O'BRIEN, C.: *Ireland: A concise history*, (3rd edn), Thames and Hudson, London, 1985.

O'CONNOR, U.: *Brien Friel: Crisis and Commitment*, Elo Publications, Dublin, 1989.
PEACOCK, A. J.: *The Achievement of Brian Friel*, Colin Smythe, Gerrards Cross, 1993.
PINE, R.: *Brian Friel and Ireland's Drama*, Routledge, London, 1990.

Background to Ireland

ANDREWS, J. H.: *A Paper Landscape: The Ordnance Survey in Nineteenth-Century Ireland*, The Clarendon Press, Oxford, 1975.
BEHAN, BRENDAN: *Richard's Cork Leg*, Eyre Methuen, London, 1973.
BELL, S. H.: *The Theatre in Ulster*, Gill and Macmillan, Dublin, 1972.
BROWN, T.: *Ireland: A Social and Cultural History, 1922–85*, Fontana Press, Glasgow, 1985.
DOWLING, P. J.: *The Hedge Schools of Ireland*, Mercier Press, Cork, 1968.
HYDE, D.: *The Literary History of Ireland*, T. Fisher Unwin, 1899.
JEFFARES, A. N.: *Anglo-Irish Literature*, Macmillan, London, 1982.
JOYCE, JAMES: *A Portrait of the Artist as a Young Man*, Penguin Books, Harmondsworth, 1969.
PAULIN, T.: *A New Look at the Language Question: Ireland and the English Crisis*, Bloodaxe Press, Newcastle-upon-Tyne, 1984.
STEINER, GEORGE: *After Babel: Aspects of Language and Translation*, Oxford University Press, London, 1975.
TODD, LORETO: *The Language of Irish Literature*, Macmillan, London, 1989.
TODD, LORETO: *Words Apart: A Dictionary of Northern Ireland English*, Colin Smythe, Gerrards Cross, 1990.
WHORF, B. L.: 'Language, thought and reality', *Selected Writings*, John B. Carroll, ed., MIT Press, Cambridge, Massachussets, 1956.
WOODHAM-SMITH, C.: *The Great Hunger*, Hamish Hamilton, London, 1962.

The author of these notes

LORETO TODD is Reader in International English at the University of Leeds. Educated in Northern Ireland and England, she has degrees in English Language, Literature and Linguistics. Dr Todd has taught in England and in West Africa, and has lectured in Australia, Canada, the Caribbean, Europe, Papua New Guinea, Singapore and the United States of America. She has published twenty-four books, including *The Language of Irish Literature* (1989), *Words Apart: A Dictionary of Northern Ireland English* (1990), *Variety in Contemporary English* (1991), *York Notes on Derek Walcott* (1993) and *A Guide to Punctuation* (1995). At present, she is on the editorial board of *English Today* and is compiling an Audio-Visual Archive of International English.